Son of the Tree

Three planets vie for
the Tree of Life!

Son of the Tree

Jack Vance

Mayflower

Granada Publishing Limited
Published in 1974 by Mayflower Books Ltd
Frogmore, St Albans, Herts AL2 2NF

First published in the USA by Ace Books Inc
Copyright © Standard Magazines Inc 1951
Made and printed in Great Britain by
Richard Clay (The Chaucer Press) Ltd
Bungay, Suffolk
Filmset in Photon Times

Son of the Tree

I

A bright penetrating chime struck into two hundred minds, broke two hundred bubbles of trance.

Joe Smith awoke without drowsiness. He was constricted, shrouded like a cocoon. He tensed, he struggled, then the spasm of alarm died. He relaxed, peered intently through the darkness.

The air was musky and humid with warm flesh — flesh of many men, above, below, to right and left, twisting, straining, fighting the elastic mesh.

Joe lay back. His mind resumed a sequence of thought left off three weeks ago. Ballenkarch? No — not yet. Ballenkarch would be farther on, farther out in the fringes. This would be Kyril, the world of the Druids.

A thin ripping sound. The hammock split along a magnetic seam. Joe eased himself out onto the cat-walk. His legs were limp as sausages and tender. There was little tone in his muscles after three weeks under hypnosis.

He walked the catwalk to the ladder, descended to the main deck, stepped out the port. At a desk sat a dark-skinned youth of sixteen, wide-eyed and smart, wearing a jumper of tan and blue pliophane. 'Name, please?'

'Joe Smith.'

The youth made a check on a list, nodded down the passage. 'First door for sanitation.'

Joe slid back the door, entered a small room thick with steam and antiseptic vapor. 'Clothes off,' bawled a brassy-voiced woman in tight trunks. She was wolf-lean — her blue-brown skin streamed with perspiration.

7

She yanked off the loose garment issued him by ship's stores — then, standing back, she touched a button. 'Eyes shut.'

Jets of cleansing solutions beat at his body. Various pressures, various temperatures, and his muscles began to waken. A blast of warm air dried him and the woman, with a careless slap, directed him to an adjoining chamber, where he shaved off his stubbly beard, trimmed his hair and finally donned the smock and sandals which appeared in a hopper.

As he left the room a steward halted him, placed a nozzle against his thigh, blew under his skin an assortment of vaccines, anti-toxins, muscle toners and stimulants. So fortified, Joe left the ship, walked out on a stage, down a ramp to the soil of Kyril.

He took a deep breath of fresh planetary air and looked about him. A sky overhung with a pearly overcast. A long gently-heaving landscape checked with tiny farms rolled away to the horizon — and there, rising like a tremendous plume of smoke, stood the Tree. The outlines were hazed by distance and the upper foliage blended with the overcast but it was unmistakable. The Tree of Life.

He waited an hour while his passport and various papers of identification were checked and counter-signed at a small glass-sided office under the embarkation stage. Then he was cleared and directed across the field to the terminal. This was a rococo structure of heavy white stone, ornately carved and beaded with intricate intaglios.

At the turnstile through the glass wall stood a Druid, idly watching the disembarkation. He was tall, nervously thin, with a pale fine ivory skin. His face was controlled, aristocratic — his hair jet-black, his eyes black and stern. He wore a glistening cuirass of enameled metal, a sumptuous robe falling in elaborate folds almost to the floor, edged with orphreys embroidered in gold thread. On his head sat an elaborate morion built of cleverly fitted cusps and planes of various metals.

Joe surrendered his passage voucher to the clerk at the turnstile desk.

'Name please.'

'It's on the voucher.'

The clerk frowned, scribbled. 'Business on Kyril?'

'Temporary visitor,' said Joe shortly. He had discussed himself, his antecedents, his business, at length with the clerk in the disembarkation office. This new questioning seemed a needless annoyance. The Druid turned his head, looked him up and down. 'Spies, nothing but spies!' He made a hissing sound under his breath, turned away.

Something in Joe's appearance aroused him. He turned back. 'You there' – in a tone of petulant irritation.

Joe turned. 'Yes?'

'Who's your sponsor? Whom do you serve?'

'No one. I'm here on my own business.'

'Do not dissemble. Everyone spies. Why pretend otherwise? You arouse me to anger. Now – whom, then, do you serve?'

'The fact of the matter is that I am not a spy,' said Joe, holding an even courtesy in his voice. Pride was the first luxury a vagrant must forego.

The Druid smiled with exaggerated thin-lipped cynicism. 'Why else would you come to Kyril?'

'Personal reasons.'

'You look to be a Thuban. What is your home world then?'

'Earth.'

The Druid cocked his head, looked at him sidewise, started to speak, halted, narrowed his eyes, spoke again. 'Do you mock me with the child's myth then – a fool's

9

paradise?'

Joe shrugged. 'You asked me a question. I answered you.'

'With an insolent disregard for my dignity and rank.'

A short plump man with a lemon-yellow skin approached with a strutting cocksure gait. He had wide innocent eyes, a pair of well-developed jowls and he wore a loose cloak of heavy blue velvet.

'An Earthman *here*?' He looked at Joe. 'You, sir?'

'That's right.'

'Then Earth is an actuality.'

'Certainly it is.'

The yellow-skinned man turned to the Druid. 'This is the second Earthman I've seen, Worship. Evidently —'

'Second?' asked Joe. 'Who was the other?'

The yellow-skinned man rolled his eyes up. 'I forget his name. Parry – Larry – Barry . . .'

'Harry? Harry Creath?'

'That's it – I'm sure of it. I had a few words with him out at Junction a year or two ago. Very pleasant fellow.'

The Druid swung on his heel, strode away. The plump man watched him go with an impassive face, then turned to Joe. 'You seem to be a stranger here '

'I just arrived.'

'Let me advise you as to these Druids. They are an emotional race, quick to anger, reckless, given to excess. And they are completely provincial, completely assured of Kyril's place as the center of all space, all time. It is wise to speak softly in their presence. May I inquire from curiosity why you are here?'

'I couldn't afford to buy passage farther.'

'And so?'

Joe shrugged. 'I'll go to work, raise some money.'

The plump man frowned thoughtfully. 'Just what talents or abilities will you use to this end?'

'I'm a good mechanic, machinist, dynamist, electrician. I can survey, work out stresses, do various odd jobs. Call myself an engineer.'

His acquaintance seemed to be considering. At last he said doubtfully, 'There is a plentiful supply of cheap labor among the Laity.'

Joe swung a glance around the terminal. 'From the look of that truss I'd say they were pretty shaky on the slide-rule.'

The other pursued his lips in dubious agreement. 'And of course the Druids are xenophobic to a high degree. A new face represents a spy.'

Joe nodded, grinned. 'I've noticed that. The first Druid I see raked me over the coals. Called me a Mang spy, whatever that is.'

The plump man nodded. 'It is what I am.'

'A Mang – or a spy?'

'Both. There is small attempt at stealth. It is admitted. Every Mang on Kyril is a spy. Likewise with the Druids on Mangtse. The two worlds are striving for dominance, economic at the moment, and there is a great deal of rancor between us.' He rubbed his chin further. 'You want a position then, with remuneration?'

'Correct,' said Joe. 'But no spying. I'm not mixing in politics. That's out. Life's too short as it is.'

The Mang made a reassuring gesture. 'Of course. Now as I mentioned the Druids are an emotional race. Devious. Perhaps we can play on these qualities. Suppose you come with me to Divinal. I have an appointment with the District Thearch and if I boast to him about the efficient technician I have taken into my service . . .' He left the rest of the sentence floating, nodded owlishly at Joe. 'This way then.'

Joe followed him through the terminal, along an

11

arcade lined with shops to a parking area. Joe glanced down the line of air-cars. Antique design, he thought – slipshod construction.

The Mang motioned him into the largest of these cars. 'To Divinal,' he told the waiting driver.

The car arose, slanted up across the gray-green landscape. For all the apparent productivity of the land the country affected Joe unpleasantly. The villages were small, cramped and the streets and alleys glistened with stagnant water. In the fields he could see teams of men – six, ten, twenty – dragging cultivators. A dreary uninspiring landscape.

'Five billion peasants,' said the Mang. 'The Laity. Two million Druids. And one Tree.'

Joe made a noncommittal sound. The Mang lapsed into silence. Farms below – interminable blocks, checks, rectangles, each a different tone of green, brown or gray. A myriad conical huts leaking smoke huddled in the corners of the fields. And ahead the Tree bulked taller, blacker, more massive.

Presently ornate white stone palaces appeared, huddled among the buttressed roots, and the car slanted down over the heavy roofs. Joe glimpsed a forest of looping balustrades, intricate panels, mullioned skylights, gargoyles, columns, embellished piers.

Then the car set down on a plat in front of a long high block of a structure, reminding Joe vaguely of the Palace at Versailles. To either side were carefully tended gardens, tessellated walks, fountains, statuary. And behind rose the Tree with its foliage hanging miles overhead.

The Mang alighted, turned to Joe. 'If you'll remove the side panel to the generator space of this car and act as if you are making a minor repair I believe you will shortly be offered a lucrative post.'

Joe said uncomfortably, 'You're going to a great deal of effort for a stranger. Are you a – philanthropist?'

The Mang said cheerfully, 'Oh no. No, *no*! I act as the whim moves me but I am not completely selfless in my acts. Let me express it this way – if I were sent to do an unspecified repair job I would take with me as wide a variety of tools as I was able.

'So, in my own – ah – mission I find that many persons have special talents or knowledges which turn out to be invaluable. Therefore I cultivate as wide and amicable an acquaintanceship as possible.'

Joe smiled thinly. 'Does it pay off?'

'Oh indeed. And then,' said the plump man blandly, 'courtesy is a reward in itself. There is an incalculable satisfaction in helpful conduct. Please don't consider yourself under obligation of any sort.'

Joe thought, without expressing himself aloud, 'I won't.'

The plump man departed, crossed the plat to a great door of carved bronze.

Joe hesitated a moment. Then, perceiving nothing to be lost by following instructions, he unclamped the side panel. A band of lead held it in place like a seal. Joe hesitated another instant, then snapped the band, lifted the panel off.

He now looked into a most amazing mechanism. It had been patched together out of spare parts, bolted with lag screws into wooden blocks, bound to the frame with bits of rope. Wires lay exposed without insulation. The force-field adjustment had been made with a wooden wedge. Joe shook his head, marveling. Then recollecting the flight from the terminal, he sweated in retrospect.

The plump yellow-skinned man had instructed him to act as if he were repairing the motor. Joe saw that pretense would be unnecessary. The powerbox was linked to

13

the metadyne by a helter-skelter tubing. Joe reached in, pulled the mess loose, reoriented the poles, connected the units with a short straight link.

Across the plat another car landed and a girl of eighteen or nineteen jumped out. Joe caught the flash of eyes in a narrow vital face as she looked toward him. Then she had left the plat.

Joe stood looking after the sapling-slender form. He relaxed, turned back to the motor. Very nice – girls were nice things. He compressed his lips, thinking of Margaret. An entirely different kind of girl was Margaret. Blonde in the first place – easy-going, flexible, but inwardly – Joe paused in his work. What was she, in her heart of hearts, where he had never penetrated?

When he had told her of his plans she had laughed, told him he was born thousands of years too late. Two years now – was Margaret still waiting? Three months was all he had thought to be gone – and then he had been led on and on, from planet to planet, out of Earth space, out across the Unicorn Gulf, out along a thin swirl of stars, beating his way from world to world.

On Jamivetta he had farmed moss on a bleak tundra and even the third-class passage to Kyril had looked good. *Margaret*, thought Joe, *I hope you're worth all this travail*. He looked at where the dark-haired Druid girl had run into the palace.

A harsh voice said, 'What's this you're doing – tearing apart the air-car? You'll be killed for such an act.'

It was the driver of the car the girl had landed in. He was a coarse-faced thick-bodied man with a swinish nose and jaw. Joe, from long and bitter experience on the outer worlds, held his tongue, turned back to investigate the machine further. He leaned forward in disbelief. Three condensers, hooked together in series, dangled and

14

swung on their connectors. He reached in, yanked off the extraneous pair, wedged the remaining condenser into a notch, hooked it up again.

'Here, here, *here*!' bellowed the driver. 'You be leaving your destructive hands off a delicate bit of mechanism!'

It was too much. Joe raised his head. 'Delicate bit of machinery! It's a wonder this pitiful tangle of junk can fly at all.'

The driver's face twisted in fury. He took a quick heavy step forward, then halted as a Druid came sweeping out on the plat – a big man with a flat red face and impressive eyebrows. He had a small hawk's-beak of a nose protruding like an afterthought between his cheeks, a mouth bracketed by ridges of stubborn muscle.

He wore a long vermilion robe with a cowl of rich black fur, an edging of fur along the robe to match. Over the cowl he wore a morion of black and green metal with a sunburst in red-and-yellow enamel cocked over one temple.

'Borandino!'

The driver cringed. 'Worship.'

'Go. Put away the Kelt.'

'Yes, Worship.'

The Druid halted before Joe. He saw the pile of discarded junk, his face became congested. 'What are you doing to my finest car?'

'Removing a few encumbrances.'

'The best mechanic on Kyril services that machinery!'

Joe shrugged. 'He's got a lot to learn. I'll put that stuff back if you want me to. It's not my car.'

The Druid stared fixedly at him. 'Do you mean to say that the car will run after you've pulled all that metal out of it?'

15

'It should run better.'

The Druid looked Joe over from head to foot. Joe decided that this must be the District Thearch. The Druid, with the faintest suggestion of furtiveness in his manner, looked back over his shoulder toward the palace, then back to Joe.

'I understand you're in the service of Hableyat.'

'The Mang? Why – yes.'

'You're not a Mang. What are you?'

Joe recalled the incident with the Druid at the terminal. 'I'm a Thuban.'

'Ah! How much does Hableyat pay you?'

Joe wished he knew something of the local currency and its value. 'Quite a bit,' he said.

'Thirty stiples a week? Forty?'

'Fifty,' said Joe.

'I'll pay you eighty,' said the Thearch. 'You'll be my chief mechanic.'

Joe nodded. 'Very well.'

'You'll come with me right now. I'll inform Hableyat of the change. You'll have no further contact with that Mang assassin. You are now a servant to the Thearch of the District.'

Joe said, 'At your service, Worship.'

II

The buzzer sounded. Joe flicked down the key, said 'Garage.'

A girl's voice issued from the plate, the peremptory self-willed voice of Priestess Elfane, the Thearch's third daughter, ringing now with an overtone Joe could not identify.

'Driver, listen very closely. Do exactly as I bid.'

'Yes, Worship.'

'Take out the black Kelt, rise to the third level, then drop back to my apartment. Be discreet and you'll profit. Do you understand?'

'Yes, Worship,' said Joe in a leaden voice.

'Hurry.'

Joe pulled on his livery Haste – discretion – stealth? A lover for Elfane? She was young but not too young. He had already performed somewhat similar errands for her sisters, Esane and Phedran. Joe shrugged. He could hope to profit. A hundred stiples, perhaps more.

He grinned ruefully as he backed the black Kelt from under the canopy. A tip from a girl of eighteen – and glad to get it. Sometime, somewhere – when he returned to Earth and Margaret – he'd dust off his pretensions to pride and dignity. They were useless to him now, a handicap.

Money was money. Money had brought him across the galaxy and Ballenkarch was at last at hand. At night when the temple searchlights left the sky he could see the sun Ballen, a bright star in the constellation the Druids called the 'Porphyrite.' The cheapest passage, hypnotized and shipped like a corpse, cost two thousand stiples.

From a salary of eighty stiples a week he was able to save seventy-five. Three weeks had passed – twenty-four more would buy him passage to Ballenkarch. Too long, with Margaret, blonde, gay, lovely, waiting on Earth. Money was money. Tips would be accepted with thanks.

Joe took the car up the palace freerise, wafting up alongside the Tree, up toward the third level. The Tree hung over him as if he had never left the ground and Joe felt the awe and wonder which three weeks in the very shadow of the trunk had done nothing to diminish.

A vast breathing sappy mass, a trunk five miles in diameter, twelve miles from the great kneed roots to the ultimate bud – the 'Vital Exprescience' in the cant of the Druids. The foliage spread out and fell away on limber boughs, each as thick through as the Thearch's palace, hung like the thatch on an old-fashioned hayrick.

The leaves were roughly triangular, three feet long – bright yellow in the upper air, darkening through lime, green, rose, scarlet, blue-black, toward the ground. The Tree ruled the horizons, shouldered aside the clouds, wore thunder and lightning like a wreath of tinsel. It was the soul of life, raw life, trampling and vanquishing the inert, and Joe understood well how it had come to be worshipped by the first marveling settlers on Kyril.

The third level. Down again, down in the black Kelt to the plat beside Priestess Elfane's apartments. Joe landed the car, jumped out, stepped across the gold-and-ivory inlay. Elfane herself slid aside the door – a vivid creature with a rather narrow face, dark, vital as a bird. She wore a simple gown of sheer white cloth without ornament and she was barefoot. Joe, who had seen her only in her official vestments, blinked, looked again with interest.

She motioned. 'This way. Hurry.' She held back the

panel and Joe entered a tall chamber, elegant but of little warmth. Bands of white marble and dark blue dumortierite surfaced two walls, bands inset with copper palettes carved with exotic birds. The third wall was hung with a tapestry depicting a group of young girls running down a grassy slope and along this wall ran a low cushioned settee.

Here sat a young man in the vesture of a Sub-Thearch – a blue robe embroidered with the red and gray orphreys of his rank. A morion inlaid with gold leaf-patterns lay beside him on the settee and a baton lathed from the Sacred Wood – an honor given only to those of Ecclesiarch degree – hung at his belt. He had lean flanks, wide spare shoulders and the most striking face of Joe's experience.

It was a narrow passionate face, wide across high cheekbones, with flat cheeks slanting down to a prow of a chin. The nose was long and straight, the forehead broad. The eyes were flat black disks in narrow expressionless sockets, the brows ink-black, the hair an ink-black mop of ringlets, artfully arranged. It was a clever, cruel face, full of fascination, overrich, overripe, without humor or sympathy – the face of a feral animal only coincidentally human.

Joe paused in mid-stride, stared into his face with instant aversion, then looked down to the corpse at the Ecclesiarch's feet – a sprawled grotesquely-rigid form oozing bright yellow blood into a crimson cloak.

Elfane said to Joe, 'This is the body of a Mangtse ambassador. A spy but nevertheless an ambassador of high rank. Someone either killed him here or brought his body here. It must not be discovered. There must be no outcry. I trust you for a loyal servant. Some very delicate negotiations with the Mang Rule are underway.

19

An incident like this might bring disaster. Do you follow me?'

Palace intrigue was none of Joe's affair. He said, 'Any orders you may give, Worship, I will follow, subject to the permission of the Thearch.'

She said impatiently, 'The Thearch is too busy to be consulted. Ecclesiarch Manaolo will assist you in conveying the corpse into the Kelt. Then you will drive us out over the ocean and we'll dispose of it.'

Joe said woodenly, 'I'll bring the car as close as possible.'

Manaolo rose to his feet, followed him to the door. Joe heard him mutter over his shoulder, 'We'll be crowded in that little cabin.'

Elfane answered impatiently, 'It's the only one I can drive.'

Joe took his time arranging the car against the door, frowning in deep thought. The only car she could drive ... He looked across fifty feet of space to the next plat along the side of the palace. A short man in a blue cloak, with hands clasped behind his back stood watching Joe benignly.

Joe reentered the room. 'There's a Mang on the next balcony.'

'*Hableyat!*' exclaimed Manaolo. He strode to the door, looked out without disclosing himself. 'He above all must not discover!'

'Hableyat knows everything,' said Elfane gloomily. 'Sometimes I think he has mastered second-sight.'

Joe knelt beside the corpse. The mouth hung open, showing a rusty orange tongue. A well-filled pouch hung at his side, half-concealed by the cloak. Joe opened it. From behind came an angry word. Elfane said, 'No, let him satisfy himself.'

Her tone, her contemptuous condescension, stung Joe.

20

But money was money. Ears burning, he reached into the pouch, pulled out a sheaf of currency. Hundred-stiple notes, a dozen at least. He returned to the pouch and found a small hand-weapon of a make he did not recognize. He tucked it into his blouse. Then he wrapped the corpse in the scarlet robe and, rising, caught hold under the armpits.

Manaolo took the ankles. Elfane went to the door. 'He's gone. Hurry!'

Five seconds saw the corpse stowed in the back. Elfane said to Joe, 'Come with me.'

Wary of turning his back on Manaolo, Joe followed. She led him into a dressing room, pointed to a pair of cases. 'Take them, load them in the back of the Kelt.'

Luggage, thought Joe. He obeyed. From the corner of his eye he saw that Hableyat had once more come out on the balcony and was smiling blandly in his direction. Joe returned inside.

Elfane was wearing sandals and a dark blue robe like a girl of the Laity. It accentuated her sprite-like appearance, the tang, the spice, which seemed an essential part of her. Joe wrenched his eyes away. Margaret would not have dealt so casually with a corpse.

He said, 'The Kelt is ready to go, Worship.'

'You will drive,' said Elfane. 'Our route will be up to the fifth level, south over Divinal, across the bay and out to sea.'

Joe shook his head. 'I'm not driving. In fact I'm not going.'

The sense of his words failed to penetrate at once. Then Elfane and Manaolo together turned their heads. Elfane was surprised with a lack of comprehension on her face rather than anger. Manaolo stood expressionless, his eyes dull, opaque.

21

Elfane said in a sharper voice, as if Joe had not understood her, 'Go on out — you will drive.'

Joe casually slid his hand inside his blouse, where the little weapon rested. Manaolo's eyes flickered, the only movement of his face, but Joe knew his mind was agile and reckless.

'I don't intend driving you,' said Joe. 'You can easily ditch that corpse without me. I don't know where you're going or why. I know I'm not going with you.'

'I order you!' exclaimed Elfane. This was fantastic, insane — contrary to the axioms of her existence.

Joe shook his head, watching warily. 'Sorry.'

Elfane dismissed the paradox from her mind. She turned to Manaolo. 'Kill him here then. *His* corpse, at least, will provoke no speculation.'

Manaolo grinned regretfully. 'I'm afraid the clobber-claw is aiming a gun at us. He will refuse to let me kill him.'

Elfane tightened her lips. 'This is ridiculous.' She whirled. Joe brought out the gun. Elfane halted stock-still, words failing in her mouth.

'Very well,' she said in a subdued voice. 'I'll give you money to be silent. Will that satisfy you?'

'Very much,' said Joe, smiling crookedly. Pride? What was pride? If it weren't for Margaret he'd enjoy . . . But no, she was plainly running off with this brilliant and dangerous Manaolo. Who would want a woman after his handling of her?

'How much?' asked Manaolo idly.

Joe calculated rapidly. He had four hundred stiples in his room, about a thousand he had taken from the corpse. He dismissed his calculations. Make it big. 'Five thousand stiples and I've forgotten everything I've seen today.'

The figure apparently did not seem exorbitant to

either of them. Manaolo felt in one pocket, then another, found a money-flap, riffled out a number of notes, tossed them to the floor.

'There's your money.'

Without a backward glance Elfane ran out on the plat, jumped into the Kelt. Manaolo strolled after her.

The Kelt jerked up, swung off into the clean air of Kyril. Joe was alone in the tall chamber.

He picked up the notes. Five thousand stiples! He went to the window, watched the air-car dwindle to a dot.

There was a small throb in his throat, a pang. Elfane was a wonderful creature. On Earth, had it not been for Margaret, he would have been entranced. But this was Kyril, where Earth was a fable. And Margaret, supple, soft, blonde as a field full of jonquils, was waiting for him to return. Or at least knew that *he* was expecting her to wait. With Margaret, Joe thought ruefully, the idea might not mean the same thing. Damn Harry Creath!

He became uneasily aware of his surroundings. Any one of a dozen persons might enter and find him. There would be difficulty explaining his presence. Somehow he had to return to his own quarters. He froze in his tracks. The sound of a door sliding brought an instant quickening of the pulse, a flush of sweat. He backed against the tapestry. Steps, slow, unhurried, came down the passage-way.

The door scraped back. A man entered the room – a short yellow-skinned man in a blue velvet cloak – Hable-yat.

III

Hableyat glanced briefly around the room, shook his head dolefully. 'A bad business. Risky for all concerned.'

Joe, standing stiffly at the wall, found ready assent. Hableyat took a couple of steps forward, peered at the floor. 'Careless. Still much blood.'

He looked up, became conscious of Joe's stance. 'But by all means be at your ease. Indeed be at your ease.' For a moment he inspected Joe impersonally. 'No doubt your mouth has been crammed with money. A marvel you still live.'

Joe said dryly, 'I was summoned here by the Priestess Elfane, who drove off in the Kelt. Otherwise I disassociate myself from the entire affair.'

Hableyat shook his head wistfully. 'If you are found here with the blood on the floor you will be questioned. And since every effort will be made to hush up Empoing's assassination you will undoubtedly be killed to insure your silence.'

Joe licked his lips. 'But isn't it from whom they want to hide the killing?'

Hableyat nodded. 'No doubt. I represent the Power and Reach of the Mangtse Dail – that is, the Bluewater Faction. Empoing was born to the Red-streams, who follow a different school of thought. They believe in a swift succession of events.'

A strange idea formed in Joe's mind and would not be dismissed. Hableyat noticed the shift of his features. His mouth, a short fleshy crevice between the two yellow jowls, drew in at the corners.

'Yes indeed. I killed him. It was necessary, believe me. Otherwise he would have slaughtered Manaolo, who is engaged on a very important mission. If Manaolo were deterred it would be – from one viewpoint – a tragedy.'

The ideas were coming too fast – they fled by Joe's mind like a school of fish past a dip-net. It was as if Hableyat were displaying a tray full of bright wares, waiting to see which Joe would select.

Joe said warily, 'Why are you telling me all this?'

Hableyat shrugged his meaty shoulders. 'Whoever you are you are no simple chauffeur.'

'Ah – but *I am*!'

'Who or what you are has not yet been established. These are complex times, when many people and many worlds want irreconcilable things and every man's origin and intentions must be closely analyzed. My information traces you to Thuban Nine, where you served as an instructor of civil engineering at the Technical Institute. From Thuban you came to Ardemizian, then to Panapol, then to Rosalinda, then to Jamivetta, finally to Kyril.

'On each planet you remained only long enough to earn transportation to the next. There is a pattern here and where there is a pattern there is a plan. Where there is a plan there is an intent and where there is an intent there are ends to be gained. And when ends are gained someone is the loser. But I see you are uneasy. Evidently you fear discovery. Am I right?'

'I do not care to be killed.'

'I suggest that we repair to my apartment, which is nearby, and then perhaps we will have a chat. I am always eager to learn and possibly in gratitude for a safe exit from this apartment —'

A chime cut him short. He started, moved rapidly to the window, looked up, down. From the window he ran to the door, listened. He motioned to Joe. 'Stand aside.'

The chime sounded again – a heavy knuckle rapped at the door. Hableyat hissed under his breath. A scratch, a scrape. The door slid aside.

A tall man with a wide red face and a little beak of a nose strode into the room. He wore a flowing white robe with a cowl and a black-green-and-gold morion atop the cowl. Hableyat slid behind him, executed a complex gesture involving a kick at the back of the man's legs, a clip of the forearm, a wrench at the wrist – and the Druid fell face down on the floor.

Joe gasped, 'It's the Thearch himself! We'll be flayed . . .'

'Come,' said Hableyat, once more a benevolent man of business. They stepped swiftly down the hall. Hableyat slid back his door. '*In.*'

Hableyat's suite was larger than the chambers of the Priestess Elfane. The sitting room was dominated by a long rectangular table, the top cut from a single slab of polished dark wood inlaid with arabesque copper leaves.

Two Mang warriors sat stiffly on each side of the door – short stocky men, craggy of feature. Hableyat paid them no heed, passed them as if they were inanimate. Noting Joe's inquiring glance, he appeared to observe them for the first time.

'Hypnotized,' he said off-handedly. 'So long as I'm in the room or the room is empty they won't move.'

Joe gingerly moved past him into the room, reflecting that he was as open to suspicion here as he was in the Priestess' apartment.

Hableyat seated himself with a grunt, motioned Joe to a chair. Rather than trust himself to a maze of unknown corridors Joe obeyed. Hableyat lay his plump palms flat on the table, fixed Joe with candid eyes.

'You appear to be caught up in an unpleasant situation, Joe Smith.'

'Not necessarily,' said Joe with a forlorn attempt at spirit. 'I could go to the Thearch, tell my story and that would be an end to it.'

Hableyat's face quivered as he chortled, opening his mouth like a squirrel. 'And then?'

Joe said nothing.

Hableyat slapped the table heartily. 'My boy, you are not yet familiar with the Druid psychology. To them killing is the response to almost any circumstance – a casual act like turning out the light on leaving a room. So when you had told your story you would be killed. For no particular reason other than that it is easier to kill than not to kill.' Hableyat idly traced the pattern of a tendril with his yellow fingernail, spoke as if musing aloud.

'Sometimes the strangest organisms are the most efficient. Kyril operates in a manner remarkable for its utter simplicity. Five billion lives devoted to feeding and pampering two million Druids and one Tree. But the system works, it perpetuates itself – which is the test for viability.

'Kyril is a grotesque ultimate of religious dedication. Laity, Druids, Tree. Laity works, Druids conduct the rites, Tree is – is immanent. Amazing! Humanity creates from the same protoplasm the clods of the Laity, the highly-tempered Druids.'

Joe stirred restlessly. 'What is all this to me?'

'I merely indicate,' said Hableyat gently, 'that your life is not worth the moist spot where I spit to anyone but yourself. What is life to a Druid? See this workmanship? The lives of ten men have been spent on this table. The slabs of marble on the wall – they were ground to fit by hand. Cost? Druids have no awareness of the concept. Labor is free, manpower unlimited.

'Even the electricity which powers and lights the palace is generated by hand in the cellars – in the name of the Tree of Life, where the poor blind souls ultimately hope to reside, serene in the sunlight and wind. The Druids thereby justify the system to their consciences, to the other worlds.

'The Laity knows nothing better. An ounce of meal, a fish, a pot of greens – so they survive. They know no marriage rites, no family, no tradition, not even folklore. They are cattle on a range. They breed with neither passion nor grace.

'Controversies? The Druid formula is simple. Kill both parties and so the controversy is dead. Unassailable – and the Tree of Life looms across the planet, the mightiest promise of life eternal the galaxy has ever known. Pure massive vitality!'

Joe hitched himself forward in his seat, looked to his right at the immobile Mang warriors. To his left, across the deep orange rug, out the window. Hableyat followed his gaze with a quizzical purse to his lips.

Joe said in a tight voice, 'Why are you keeping me here? What are you waiting for?'

Hableyat blinked rapidly, reproachfully. 'I am conscious of no intent to detain you. You are free to leave any time you wish.'

'Why bring me here in the first place?' demanded Joe.

Hableyat shrugged. 'Sheer altruism possibly. If you returned to your quarters now you are as good as dead. Especially after the regrettable intrusion of the Thearch.'

Joe relaxed into the chair. 'That's not – necessarily true.'

Hableyat nodded vigorously. 'I'm afraid it is. Consider – it is known or will be known, that you took up the black Kelt, which subsequently was driven away by

Priestess Elfane and Ecclesiarch Manaolo. The Thearch, coming to his daughter's apartments, perhaps to investigate, perhaps in response to a summons, is attacked. Shortly afterwards the chauffeur returns to his quarters.' He paused, opened plump hands out significantly.

Joe said, 'All right then. What's on your mind?'

Hableyat tapped the table with his fingernail. 'These are complex times, complex times. You see,' he added confidentially, 'Kyril is becoming overpopulated with Druids.'

Joe frowned. 'Overpopulated? With two million Druids?'

Hableyat laughed. 'Five billion Laity are unable to provide a dignified existence for more. You must understand that these poor wretches have no interest in producing. Their single aspiration is to pass through life as expeditiously as possible so as to take their place as a leaf on the Tree.

'The Druids are caught in a dilemma. To increase production they must either educate and industrialize — thus admitting to the Laity that life offers pleasures other than rapt contemplation — or they must find other sources of wealth and production. To this end the Druids have decided to operate a bank of industries on Ballenkarch. So we Mangs and our highly industrialized world become involved. We see in the Druid plan a threat to our own well being.'

Joe asked with an air of tired patience, 'How does this involve *me*?'

'My job as emissary-at-large,' said Hableyat, 'is to promote the interests of my world. To this end I require a great deal of information. When you arrived here a month ago you were investigated. You were traced back as far as a planet of the distant sun Thuban. Before that, your trail eludes us.'

Joe said with incredulous anger, 'But you *know* my home world! I told you the first time I saw you. Earth. And you said that you had spoken to another Earthman, Harry Creath.'

Hableyat nodded briskly. 'Exactly. But it has occurred to me that "Earth" as a place of origin offers a handy anonymity.' He peered at Joe slyly. 'Both for you and Harry Creath.'

Joe took a deep breath. 'You know more of Harry Creath than you let me believe.'

Hableyat appeared surprised that Joe should consider this fact exceptional. 'Of course. It is necessary for me to know many things. Now this "Earth" you speak of — is its identity actually more than verbal?' And he eyed Joe inquisitively.

'I assure you it is,' said Joe, heavily sarcastic. 'You people are so far out along this little wisp of stars that you've forgotten the rest of the universe.'

Hableyat nodded, drummed his fingers on the table. 'Interesting, interesting. This brings a rather new emphasis to light.'

Joe said impatiently, 'I'm not aware of any emphasis, either old or new. My business, such as it is, is personal. I have no interest in your enterprises and least of all do I want to become involved.'

There was a harsh pounding at the door. Hableyat rose to his feet with a grunt of satisfaction. This was what he had been awaiting, Joe thought.

'I repeat,' said Hableyat, 'that you have no choice. You are involved in spite of any wish to the contrary. Do you want to live?'

'Of course I want to live.' Joe half-rose to his feet as the pounding was resumed.

'Then agree to whatever I say — no matter how far-fetched it may seem to you. Do you understand?'

'Yes,' said Joe with resignation.

Hableyat spoke a sharp word. The two warriors bounded to their feet like mechanical men, 'Open the door.'

The door slid back. The Thearch stood in the opening, his face wrathful. Behind him stood a half dozen Druids in robes of different colors – Ecclesiarchs, Sub-Thearchs, Presbytes, Hierophants.

Hableyat was transformed. His overt characteristics became intensified. His benignity softened to obsequiousness; his bland ease of manner became a polished unction. He trotted forward as if the Thearch's visit afforded him tremendous pride and delight.

The Thearch towered in the doorway, glaring up and down the room. His eyes passed over the two warriors, came to rest on Joe.

He raised a hand, pointed portentously. 'There's the man! A murderous blackguard! Lay hold, we'll see the end of him before the hour's out.'

The Druids swept forward in a swift rustle of robes. Joe reached for his weapon. But the two Mang warriors, moving so deftly and easily that they seemed not to have moved at all, blocked the doorway. A hot-eyed Druid in a brown-and-green robe reached to thrust them aside.

There was a twinkle of blue light, a crackle, a startled exclamation and the Druid leapt back, trembling in indignation. 'He's charged with static!'

Hableyat bustled forward, all dismay and alarm. 'Your Worship, what is happening?'

The Thearch's expression was vastly contemptuous. 'Stand aside, Mang, call off your electrified go-devils. I'll have that man.'

Cried Hableyat, 'But Worship, Worship – you dismay

me. Can it be that I've taken a criminal into my service?'

'*Your* service?'

'Surely your Worship is aware that in order to pursue a realistic policy my government employs a number of unofficial observers?'

'Cutthroat spies!' roared the Thearch.

Hableyat rubbed his chin. 'If such is the case, your Worship, I am disillusioned, since the Druid spies on Mangtse are uniformly self-effacing. Just what is my servant accused of?'

The Thearch thrust his head forward, said with soft fervor, 'I'll tell you what he's done – he's killed one of your own men – a Mang! There's yellow blood all over the floor of my daughter's chamber. Where there's blood, there's death.'

'Your Worship!' exclaimed Hableyat. 'This is serious news! Who is it that is dead?'

'How do I know? Enough that there's a man killed and that this —'

'But your Worship! This man has been in my company all day. Your news is alarming. It means that a representative of my government has been attacked. I fear that there will be tumult in the Lathbon. Where did you notice this blood? In the chamber of your daughter, the Priestess? Where is she? Perhaps she can shed some light on the matter.'

'I don't know where she is.' He turned, pointed a finger. 'Alamaina – find the Priestess Elfane. I wish to speak to her.' Then to Hableyat, 'Do I understand that you are taking this blackguard spy under your protection?'

Hableyat said courteously, 'Our security officers have been solicitous in guarding the safety of the Druids representing your Worship on Mangtse.'

The Thearch turned on his heel, strode off through

the hooded forms of his Druids.

Joe said, 'So now I'm a Mang spy.'

'What would you have?' inquired Hableyat.

Joe returned to his seat. 'For some reason I can't imagine you are determined to attach me to your staff.'

Hableyat made a gesture of deprecation.

Joe stared at him a moment. 'You murder your own men, you strike down the Thearch in his daughter's sitting-room – and somehow I find myself held to account for it. It's not possible that you planned it that way?'

'Now, now, now,' murmured Hableyat.

Joe asked politely, 'May I presume upon your courtesy further?'

'Certainly. By all means.' Hableyat waited attentively.

Joe said boldly, without any real expectation of Hableyat's assent, 'Take me to the Terminal. Put me on the packet to Ballenkarch which leaves today.'

Hableyat, raising his eyebrows sagely, nodded. 'A very reasonable request – and one which I would be unkind to deny. Are you ready to leave at once?'

'Yes,' said Joe dryly, 'I am.'

'And you have sufficient funds?'

'I have five thousand stiples given me by the Priestess Elfane and Manaolo.'

'Hah! I see. They were anxious then to be on their way.'

'I received that impression.'

Hableyat looked up sharply. 'There is suppressed emotion in your voice.'

'The Druid Manaolo arouses a great deal of aversion in me.'

'*Hah!*' said Hableyat with a sly wink. 'And the Priestess arouses a great deal of the opposite? Oh, you youngsters! If only I had my youth back how I would enjoy myself!'

Joe said in precise tones. 'My future plans involve neither Manaolo nor Elfane.'

'Only the future can tell,' intoned Hableyat. 'Now then – to the Terminal.'

IV

There was no signal which Joe could perceive but in three minutes, during which Hableyat sat silently hunched in a chair, a heavy well-appointed air-car swung alongside the plat. Joe went cautiously to the window, looked along the side of the Palace. The sun was low. Shadows from the various balconies, landing stages, carved work, ran obliquely along the stone, creating a confusion of shape in which almost anything might be hidden.

Below were the garage and his cubicle. Nothing there of value – the few hundred stiples he had saved from his salary as chauffeur he dismissed. Beyond rose the Tree, a monstrous mass his eye could not encompass at one glance. To see edge to edge he had to turn his head from right to left. The shape was uncertain from this close distance of a mile or so. A number of slow-swinging members laden with foliage overhung the Palace.

Hableyat joined him at the window. 'It grows and grows. Some day it will grow beyond its strength or the strength of the ground. It will buckle and fall in the most terrible sound yet heard on the planet. And the crash will be the crack of doom for the Druids.'

He glanced carefully up and down the face of the Palace. 'Now walk swiftly. Once you are in the car you are safe from any hidden marksmen.'

Again Joe searched the shadows. Then gingerly he stepped out on the plat. It seemed very wide, very empty. He crossed to the car with a naked tingling under his skin. He stepped through the door and the car swayed under him. Hableyat bounced in beside him.

'Very well, Juliam,' said Hableyat to the driver, a very old Mang, sad-eyed, wrinkled of face, his hair gone brindle-brown with age. 'We'll be off – to the Terminal. Stage Four, I believe. The *Belsaurion* for Junction and Ballenkarch.'

Juliam trod on the elevator pedal. The car swung up and away. The Palace dwindled below and they rose beside the dun trunk of the Tree, up under the first umbrella of fronds.

The air of Kyril was usually filled with a smoky haze but today the slanting sun shone crisply through a perfectly clear atmosphere. The city Divinal, such as it was – a heterogeneity of palaces, administrative offices, temples, a few low warehouses – huddled among the roots of the Tree and quickly gave way to a gently rolling plain thronged with farms and villages.

Roads converged in all directions toward the Tree and along these roads walked the drab men and women of the Laity – making their pilgrimage to the Tree. Joe had watched them once or twice as they entered the Ordinal Cleft, a gap between two great arched roots. Tiny figures like ants, they paused, turned to stare out across the gray land before continuing on into the Tree. Every day brought thousands from all corners of Kyril, old and young. Wan dark-eyed men, aflame for the peace of the Tree.

They crossed a flat plain covered with small black capsules. To one side a mass of naked men performed calisthenics – jumping, twisting in perfect time.

Hableyat said, 'There you see the Druid space-navy.'

Joe looked sharply to see if he were indulging in sarcasm, but the pudgy face was immobile.

'They are well suited to the defense of Kyril, which is to say, the Tree. Naturally anyone wishing to defeat the

Druids by violence would think to destroy the Tree, thus demolishing the morale of the natives. But in order to destroy the Tree a flotilla must approach relatively close to Kyril, say within a hundred thousand miles, for any accuracy of bombardment.

'The Druids maintain a screen of these little boats a million miles out. They're crude but very fast and agile. Each is equipped with a warhead – in fact they are suicide boats and to date they are admitted to be an affective defense for the Tree.'

Joe sat a moment in silence. Then, 'Are these boats made here? On Kyril?'

'They are quite simple,' said Hableyat with veiled contempt. 'A shell, a drive, an oxygen tank. The Lay soldiers are not expected to demand or appreciate comfort. There's a vast number of these little boats. Why not? Labor is free. The idea of cost has no meaning for the Druids. I believe the control equipment is imported from Beland and likewise the firing release. Otherwise the boats are hand-made here on Kyril.'

The field full of beetle-boats slanted, faded astern. Ahead appeared the thirty-foot wall surrounding the Terminal. The long glass station stretched along one side of the rectangle. Along another was a line of palatial mansions – the consular offices of off-planets.

Across the field, in the fourth of five bays, a medium-sized combination freight–passenger vessel rested and Joe saw that it was ready to take off. The cargo hatch had been battened, the loading trams swung back and only a gangplank connected the ship with the ground.

Juliam set the car down in a parking area to the side of the station. Hableyat put a restraining hand on Joe's arm.

'Perhaps – for your own safety – it might be wise if I arranged your passage. The Thearch might have planned some sort of trouble. One never knows where these unpredictable Druids are concerned.' He hopped out of the car. 'If you'll remain here then — out of sight — I'll return very shortly.'

'But the money for the passage —'

'A trifle, a trifle,' said Hableyat. 'My government has more money than it knows how to spend. Allow me to invest two thousand stiples toward a fund of good will with our legendary Mother Earth.'

Joe relaxed dubiously into the seat. Two thousand stiples was two thousand stiples and it would help him on his way back to Earth. If Hableyat thought to hold him under obligation Hableyat was mistaken. He stirred in his seat. Better get out while the getting was good. Things like this did not happen without some unpleasant *quid pro quo*. He raised a hand toward the door and met Juliam's eye. Juliam shook his head.

'No, no, sir. Lord Hableyat will be back at once and his wishes were that you remain out of sight.'

In a spasm of defiance, Joe said, 'Hableyat can wait.'

He jumped from the car and, ignoring Juliam's querulous voice, strode off toward the station. His anger cooled as he walked and in his green-white-and-black livery he felt conspicuous. Hableyat had a rude habit of being consistently right.

A sign across the walk read, *Costumes of all worlds. Change here. Arrive at your destination in a fitting garb.*

Joe stepped in. Through the glass window he would be able to see Hableyat if he left the station, returning to the car. The proprietor stood quietly at his command, a tall bony man of nameless race with a wide waxy face, wide guileless eyes of pale blue.

'My Lord wishes?' he inquired in even tones which ignored the servant's livery which Joe was stripping off.

'Get rid of these. Give me something suitable for Ballenkarch.'

The shop-keeper bowed. He ran a grave eye over Joe's form, turned to a rack, brought forward a set of garments which made Joe blink — red pantaloons, a tight blue sleeveless jacket, a voluminous white blouse. Joe said doubtfully, 'That's not quite — it's not subdued, is it?'

'It is a typical Ballenkarch costume, my Lord – typical, that is to say, among the more civilized clans. The savages wear skins and sacks.' He twisted the garments to display front and back. 'As it is, it denotes no particular rank. A vavasour hangs a sword at his left side. A grandee of the Vail Alan Court wears a chap-band of black in addition. The Ballenkarch costumes, Lord, are marked by a rather barbaric flamboyance.'

Joe said, 'Give me a plain gray traveling suit. I'll change to Ballenkarch style when I arrive.'

'As you wish, Lord.'

The traveling suit was more to his liking. With deep satisfaction Joe zipped close the seams, snugged the ankles and wrists, belted the waist.

'And what style morion, Lord?'

Joe grimaced. Morions were *comme il faut* among the rank of Kyril. Laymen, louts, menials, were denied the affectation of a glistening complex morion. He pointed to a low shell of bright metal with a sweeping rake-shell brim. 'That one if it will fit.'

The shopkeeper bent his form almost into an inverted U. 'Yes, your Worship.'

Joe glanced at him sharply, then considered the morion he had selected — a glistening beautiful helmet, useful for nothing other than decorative headdress. It was rather like the one Ecclesiarch Manaolo had worn. He shrugged, jammed it on his head, transferred the contents of his pockets. Gun, money, wallet with identification papers. 'How much do I owe you?'

'Two hundred stiples, your Worship.'

Joe gave him a pair of notes, stepped out on the arcade. As he walked it occurred to him that his step was firmer, that in fact he was swaggering. The change from livery into the gray suit and swashbuckling morion had altered the color of his psychology. Morale, confidence, will-to-win — they were completely intangible, yet so ultimately definite. Now to find Hableyat.

There was Hableyat ahead of him, walking arm in arm with a Mang in green-blue-and-yellow uniform, speaking very earnestly, very expressively. Joe wished he were able to read lips. The two stopped at the ramp down to the field. The Mang officer bowed curtly, turned, marched back along the arcade. Hableyat ambled down the ramp, started across the field.

It occurred to Joe that he would like to hear what Juliam said to Hableyat and Hableyat's comments on his absence. If he ran to the end of the arcade, jumped the wall, ran around behind the parking lot, he would be able to approach the car from the rear, probably unseen.

Suiting action to thought he turned, raced the length of the terrace, heedless of startled glances. Lowering himself to the blue-green turf he dodged close to the wall, kept as many of the parked cars as possible between himself and the leisurely Hableyat. He reached the car, flung himself to his hands and knees unseen by Juliam, who had his eyes on Hableyat.

Juliam slid back the door. Hableyat said cheerfully, 'Now then, my friend, everything is —' He stopped. Then sharply to Juliam, 'Where is he? Where has he gone?'

'He left,' said Juliam, 'a little after you did.'

Hableyat muttered a pungent syllable. 'The confounded unpredictability of the man! I gave him strict instructions to remain here.'

Juliam said, 'I reminded him of your instructions. He ignored me.'

'That's the difficulty,' said Hableyat, 'in dealing with men of limited intellect. They cannot be trusted for logical performance. A thousand times would I prefer to wrestle with a genius. His methods, at least, would be understandable. . . . If Erru Kametin sees him all my plans will be defeated. Oh,' he groaned, 'the bull-headed fool!'

Juliam sniffed but held his tongue. Hableyat spoke incisively. 'You go – look along the arcade. If you see him send him back quickly. I'll wait here. Then telephone Erru Kametin – he'll be at the Consulate. Identify yourself as Aglom Fourteen. He will inquire further and you will reveal that you were an agent for Empoing, who is now dead – that you have important information for his ears.

'He will wish you to appear but you will profess fear of Druid counteraction. You will tell him that you have definitely identified the courier, that he will be traveling with the article in question on the *Belsaurion*. You will give a quick description of this man and then return here.'

'Yes, Lord.'

Joe heard the shuffle of Juliam's feet. He slid back, ducked behind a long blue carryall, rose to his feet. He saw Juliam cross the field, then by a roundabout route he returned to the car, entered.

Hableyat's eyes were glittering but he said in a careless tone, 'So there you are, young man. Where have you been? . . . Ah, new garments, I see. Very wise, very wise, though of course it was rash to appear along the arcade.'

He reached into his pouch, came out with an envelope. 'Here is your ticket, Ballenkarch via Junction.'

'Junction? What or where is Junction?'

Hableyat put the tips of his fingers together, said in a tone of exaggerated precision, 'Kyril, Mangtse and Ballenkarch, as you may be aware, form a triangle approximately equilateral. Junction is an artificial satellite at its center. It is also situated along the Mangtse–Thombol–Beland traffic lane and, at a perpendicular, along the Frums–Outer System passage and so makes a very convenient way station or transfer point.

'It is an interesting place from many aspects. The unique method of construction, the extremities of the efforts made to entertain visitors, the famous Junction Gardens, the cosmopolitan nature of the people encountered there. I'm sure you will find it an interesting voyage.'

'I imagine I shall,' said Joe.

'There will be spies aboard – everywhere, indeed, there are spies. One cannot move his foot without kicking a spy. Their instructions in regard to you may or may not include violence. I counsel the utmost vigilance – though, as is well known, a skillful assassin cannot be denied opportunity.'

Joe said with grim good-humor, 'I've got a gun.'

Hableyat met his eyes with limpid innocence. 'Good – excellent. Now the ship leaves almost any minute. You had better get aboard. I won't go with you but wish you good luck from here.'

Joe jumped to the ground. 'Thanks for your efforts,' he said evenly.

Hableyat raised a monitory hand. 'No thanks, please. I'm glad that I'm able to assist a fellow-man when he's in trouble. Although there is a slight service I'd like you to render me. I've promised my friend, the Prince of Ballenkarch, a sample of the lovely Kyril heather and perhaps you will convey him this little pot with my regards.'

Hableyat displayed a plant growing in an earthenware pot. 'I'll put it in this bag. Please be careful with it. Water it once a week if you will.'

Joe accepted the potted plant. A hoot from the ship's horn rang across the field. 'Hurry then,' said Hableyat. 'Perhaps we'll meet again some day.'

'Goodby,' said Joe. He turned, walked toward the ship, anxious now to embark.

Last-minute passengers were crossing the field from the station. Joe stared at a couple not fifty feet distant — a tall broad-shouldered young man with the face of a malicious satyr, a slender dark-haired girl — Manaolo and the Priestess Elfane.

V

The skeleton-work of the embarkation stage made a black web on the overcast sky. Joe climbed the worn plank stairs to the top deck. No one was behind. No one observed him. He reached under an L-beam, set the potted plant on the flange out of sight. Whatever it was, it was dangerous. He wanted nothing to do with it. Hableyat's *quid pro quos* might come high.

Joe smiled sourly. 'Limited intellect' and 'bull-headed fool' – there was an ancient aphorism, to the effect that eavesdroppers hear no good of themselves. It seemed to apply in his own case.

Joe thought, *I've been called worse things. And once I get to Ballenkarch it won't make any difference. . . .*

Ahead of him Manaolo and Elfane crossed the stage, straight ahead with that fixed and conscious will characteristic of the Druids. They climbed the gangplank, turned into the ship. Joe grimaced. Elfane's slim legs twinkling up the stairs had sent sweet-sour chills along his nerves. And the proud back of Manaolo – it was like taking two drugs with precisely opposite effects.

Joe cursed old Hableyat. Did he imagine that Joe would be so obsessed with infatuation for the Priestess Elfane as to challenge Manaolo? Joe snorted. *Overripe old hypocrite!* In the first place he had no slightest intimation that Elfane would consider him as a lover. And after Manaolo's handling of her – his stomach muscles twisted. Even, he amended dutifully, if his loyalty to Margaret would permit his interest. He had enough problems of his own without inviting others.

At the gangplank stood a steward in a red skin-tight uniform. Rows of trefoil gold frogs decorated his legs, a radio was clamped to his ear with a mike pressed to his throat. He was a member of a race strange to Joe – white-haired, loose-jointed, with eyes as green as emeralds.

Joe felt the tenseness rising up in himself, if the Thearch suspected that he were on his way off-planet, now he would be stopped.

The steward took his ticket, nodded courteously, motioned him within. Joe crossed the gangplank to the convex black hulk, entered the shadowed double port. At a temporary desk sat the purser, another man of the white-haired race. Like the steward he wore a scarlet suit which seemed like a second skin. In addition he wore glass epaulets and a small scarlet skullcap.

He extended a book to Joe. 'Your name and thumb-print, please. They waive responsibility for accidents incurred on route.'

Joe signed, pressed his thumb on the indicated square while the purser examined his ticket. 'First class passage, Cabin 14. Luggage, Worship?'

'I have none,' said Joe. 'I imagine there's a ship's store where I can buy linen.'

'Yes, your Worship, yes indeed. Now, if you'll kindly step to your cabin, a steward will secure you for take-off.'

Joe glanced down at the book he had signed. Immediately before his signature he read in a tall angular hand, *Druid Manaolo kia Benlodieth*, and then in a round backhand script, *Alnietho kia Benlodieth*. Signed as his wife – Joe chewed at his lip. Manaolo was assigned to Cabin 12, Elfane to 13.

Not strange in itself. These freighter–passenger ships, unlike the great passenger packets flashing out from Earth in every direction, offered little accommodation for passengers. Cabins, so-called, were closets with hammocks, drawers, tiny collapsible bathroom facilities.

A steward in the skin-tight garment, this time a firefly blue, said, 'This way, Lord Smith.'

Joe thought – to excite reverence all a man needed was a tin hat.

He followed the steward past the hold, where the steerage passengers already lay entranced and bundled into their hammocks, then through a combination saloon–dining room. The far wall was faced with two tiers of doors, with a web-balcony running under the second tier. No. 14 was the last door on the top row.

As the steward led Joe past No. 13 the door was thrust aside and Manaolo came bursting out. His face was pale, his eyes widened to curious elliptical shape, showing the full disk of the dead black retinas. He was plainly in a blind fury. He shouldered Joe aside, opened the door to No. 12, passed within.

Joe slowly pulled himself back from the rail. For an instant all sense, all reason, had left him. It was a curious sensation – one unknown to him before. An unlimited elemental aversion which even Harry Creath had never aroused. He turned slowly back along the catwalk.

Elfane stood in the door of her cabin. She had removed the blue cloak and stood in her soft white dress – a dark-haired girl with a narrow face, mobile and alive, now clenched in anger. Her eyes met Joe's. For an instant they stared eye to eye, faces two feet apart.

The hate in Joe's heart moved over for another emotion, a wonderful lift into clean air, a delight, a ferment. Her eyebrows contracted in puzzlement, she half-opened her mouth to speak. Joe wondered with a queer sinking feeling, if she recognized him? Their previous contacts had been so careless, so impersonal. He was a new man in his new clothes.

She turned, shut the door, Joe continued to No. 14, where the steward webbed him into his hammock for the take-off.

Joe awoke from the take-off trance. He said, 'Whatever you're looking for, I haven't got it. Hableyat gave you a bum steer.'

The man across the cabin froze into stillness, back turned toward Joe.

Joe said, 'Don't move, I've got my gun on you.'

He jerked up from the hammock but the webbing held him. At the sound of his efforts the intruder stole a glance over his shoulder, ducked, slid from the cabin like a ghost.

Joe called out harshly but there was no sound. Throwing off the web he ran to the door, looked out into the saloon. It was empty.

Joe turned back, shut the door. Waking from the trance he had no clear picture of his visitor. A man short and stocky, moving on joints set at curious splayed angles. There had been a flashing glimpse of the man's face but all Joe could recall was a sallow yellow tinge as if the underlying blood ran bright yellow. A Mang.

Joe thought, *Now it's starting. Damn Hableyat, setting me up as his stalking horse!* He considered reporting to the captain, who, neither Druid nor Mang, might be unsympathetic to lawlessness aboard his ship. He decided against the action. He had nothing to report – merely a prowler in his cabin. The captain would hardly put the entire passenger list through a psycho-reading merely to apprehend a prowler.

Joe rubbed his face, yawned. Out in space once more on the last leg of his trip. Unless, of course, Harry had moved on again.

He raised the stop-ray shield in front of the port,

looked out into space. Ahead, in the direction of flight, a buffer-screen absorbed what radiation the ship either overtook or met. Otherwise the energy, increased in frequency and hardness by the Doppler action due to the ship's velocity, would have crisped him instantly.

Light impinging from a beam showed him stars more or less with their normal magnitudes, the perspectives shifting and roiling as he watched – and the stars floating, eddying, drifting like motes in a beam of light. To the stern was utter darkness – no light could overtake the vessel. Joe dropped the shutter. The scene was familiar to him. Now for a bath, his clothes, food. . . .

Looking at his face in the mirror he noticed a stubble of beard. The shaver lay on a glass shelf over the collapsible sink. Joe reached – yanked his hand to a halt, an inch from the shaver. When first he had entered the cabin it had hung from a clasp on the bulkhead.

Joe eased himself away from the wall, his nerves tingling. Certainly his visitor had not been shaving? He looked down to the deck – saw a mat of coiled woven brass. Bending, he noticed a length of copper wire joining the mat to the drain pipe.

Gingerly he scooped the shaver into his shoe, carried it to his bunk. A metal band circled the handle with a tit entering the case near the unit which scooped power from the ship's general field.

In the long run, thought Joe, he had Hableyat to thank – Hableyat who had so kindly rescued him from the Thearch and put him aboard the *Belsaurion* with a potted plant.

Joe rang for the steward. A young woman came, white-haired like the other members of the crew. She wore a parti-colored short-skirted garment of orange and blue that fitted her like a coat of paint. Joe dumped the shaver into a pillowcase. He said, 'Take this to the

51

electrician. It's very dangerous – got a short in it. Don't touch it. Don't let anyone touch it. And – will you please bring me another shaver?'

'Yes, sir.' She departed.

Finally bathed, shaved and as well-dressed as his limited wardrobe permitted, he sauntered out into the saloon, stepping high in the ship's half-gravity. Four or five men and women sat along the lounges to the side, engaging in guarded conversation.

Joe stood watching a moment. Peculiar, artificial creatures, he thought, these human beings of the Space Age – brittle and so completely formal that conversation was no more than an exchange of polished mannerisms. So sophisticated that nothing could shock them as much as naïve honesty.

Three Mangs sat in the group – two men, one old, the other young, both wearing the rich uniforms of the Mangtse Red-Branch. A young Mang woman with a certain heavy beauty, evidently the wife of the young officer. The other couple, like the race which operated the ship, were human deviants unfamiliar to Joe. They were like pictures he had seen in a childhood fairybook – wispy fragile creatures, big-eyed, thin-skinned, dressed in loose sheer gowns.

Joe descended the stairs to the main deck and a ship's officer, the head steward presumably, appeared. Gesturing politely to Joe he spoke to the entire group. 'I present Lord Joe Smith of the planet' – he hesitated – 'the planet Earth.'

He turned to the others in the group. 'Erru Kametin' – this was the older of the two Mang officers – 'Erru Ex Amma and Erritu Thi Amma, of Mangtse.' He turned to the fairy-like creatures. 'Prater Luli Hassimassa and his lady Hermina of Cil.'

Joe bowed politely, seated himself at the end of the lounge. The young Mang oficer, Erru Ex Amma, asked curiously, 'Did I understand that you claim *Earth* for your home planet?'

'Yes,' said Joe half-truculently. 'I was born on the continent known as North America, where the first ship ever to leave Earth was built.'

'Strange,' muttered the Mang, eyeing Joe with an expression just short of disbelief. 'I've always considered talk of Earth one of the superstitions of space, like the Moons of Paradise and the Star Dragon.'

'I can assure you that Earth is no legend,' said Joe. 'Somehow in the outward migrations, among the wars and the planetary programs of propaganda, the real existence of Earth has been called to question. And we travel very rarely into this outer swirl of the galaxy.'

The fairy-woman spoke in a piping voice which suited her moth-frail appearance. 'And you maintain that all of us — you, the Mangs, we Cils, the Belands who operate the ship, the Druids, the Frumsans, the Thablites — they are *all* ultimately derived from Earth stock?'

'Such is the fact.'

A metallic voice said, 'That is not entirely true. The Druids were the first fruit of the Tree of Life. That is the well-established doctrine, and any other allegation is false.'

Joe said in a careful voice, 'You are entitled to your belief.'

The steward came forward. 'Ecclesiarch Manaolo kia Benlodieth of Kyril.'

There was a moment of silence after the introductions. Then Manaolo said, 'Not only am I entitled to my belief, but I must protest the propagation of incorrect statements.'

'That also is your privilege,' said Joe. 'Protest all you like.'

He met Manaolo's dead black eyes and there seemed no human understanding behind them, no thought – only emotion and obstinate will.

There was movement behind; it was Priestess Elfane. She was presented to the company and without words she settled beside Hermina of Cil. The atmosphere now had changed and even though she but murmured pleasantries with Hermina her presence brought a piquancy, a sparkle, a spice . . .

Joe counted. Eight with himself – fourteen cabins – six passengers yet unaccounted for. One of the thirteen had tried to kill him – a Mang.

A pair of Druids issued from cabins two and three, and were introduced – elderly sheep-faced men en route to a mission on Ballenkarch. They carried with them a portable alter, which they immediately set up in a corner of the saloon, and began a series of silent rites before a small representation of the Tree. Manaolo watched them without interest a moment or two, then turned away.

Four unaccounted for, thought Joe.

The steward announced the first meal of the day, and at this moment another couple appeared from their cabins, two Mangs in non-military attire – loose wrappings of colored silk, light cloaks, jeweled corselets. They bowed formally to the company and, since the steward was arranging the collapsible table, they took their places without introduction. Five Mangs, thought Joe. Two soldiers, two civilians, a woman. Two cabins still concealed their occupants.

Cabin No. 10 opened, and an aged woman of extreme height stepped slowly out on the balcony. She was bald as an egg and her head was flat on top. She had a great bony nose, black bulging eyes. She wore a black cape and on each finger of both hands was a tremendous jewel.

One more to go. The door to cabin No. 6 remained closed.

The meal was served from a menu surprisingly varied, to serve the palates of many races. Joe, in his planet-to-planet journey across the galaxy, perforce had dismissed all queasiness. He had eaten organic matter of every conceivable color, consistency, odor and flavor.

Familiar items he could put a name to – ferns, fruits, fungus, roots, reptiles, insects, fish, mollusks, slugs, eggs, spore-sacs, animals and birds – and at least as many objects he could neither define nor recognize and whose sole claim to his appetite lay in the example of others.

His place at the table was directly opposite Manaolo and Elfane. He noticed that they did not speak and several times he felt her eyes on him, puzzled, appraising, half-furtive. *She's sure she's seen me*, thought Joe, *but she can't remember where.*

After the meal the passengers separated. Manaolo retired to the gymnasium behind the saloon. The five Mangs sat down to a game played with small rods of different colors. The Cils went up to the promenade along the back rib of the ship. The tall demon-woman sat in a chair, gazing blankly into nothingness.

Joe would likewise have taken exercise in the gymnasium but the presence of Manaolo deterred him. He selected a film from the ship's library, prepared to return to his room.

Priestess Elfane said in a low voice, 'Lord Smith, I wish to speak to you.'

'Certainly.'

'Will you come to my room?'

Joe looked over his shoulder. 'Won't your husband be annoyed?'

'Husband?' She managed to inject an enormous weight of contempt and angry disgust into her voice. 'The relationship is purely nominal.' She stopped, looked away, apparently regretting her words. Then she continued in a cool voice, 'I wish to speak to you.' She turned away, marched for her cabin.

Joe chuckled quietly. The vixen knew no other world than that in her own brain, had no conception that wills could exist in opposition to hers. Amusing now — but what a devil when she grew older! It occurred to Joe that it would be a pleasant experience to be lost with her on an uninhabited planet — taming her willfulness, opening up her consciousness.

He leisurely followed to her cabin. She sat on the bunk. He took a seat on the bench. 'Well?'

'You say your home is the planet Earth — the mythical Earth. Is that true?'

'Yes, it's true.'

'Where is Earth?'

'In toward the Center, perhaps a thousand light-years.'

'What is Earth like?' She leaned forward, elbow on her knee, chin on her hand, watching him with interested eyes.

Joe, suddenly flustered, shrugged. 'You ask a question I can't answer in a word. Earth is a world of great age. Everywhere are ancient buildings, ancient cities, traditions. In Egypt stand the Great Pyramids, built by the first civilized men. In England a circle of chipped stones, Stonehenge, are replicas of a race almost as old. In the caves of France and Spain, far underground, are drawings of animals, scratched by men hardly removed from the beasts they hunted.'

She drew a deep breath. 'But your cities, your civilization – are they different from ours?'

Joe put on a judicious expression. 'Naturally they are different. No two planets are alike. Ours is an old stable culture – mellowed, kindly. Our races have merged – I am the result of their mingling. In these outer regions men have been blocked off and separated and have specialized once again. You Druids, who are very close to us physically, correspond to the ancient Caucasian race of the Mediterranean branch.'

'But do you have no Great God – no Tree of Life?'

'At present,' said Joe, 'there is no organized religion on Earth. We are free to express our joy at being alive in any way which pleases us. Some revere a cosmic creator – others merely acknowledge the physical laws controlling the universe to almost the same result. The worship of fetishes, anthropoid, animal or vegetable – like your Tree – has long been extinct.'

She sat up sharply. 'You – you deride our sacred institution.'

'Sorry.'

She rose to her feet, then sat down, swallowing her wrath. 'You interest me in many ways,' she said sullenly, as if justifying her forbearance to herself. 'I have the peculiar feeling that you are known to me.'

Joe, on a half-sadistic impulse, said, 'I was your father's chauffeur. Yesterday you and your – husband were planning to kill me.'

She froze into unblinking rigidity, staring, mouth half-open. Then she relaxed, shuddered, shrank back. '*You* – are you —'

But Joe had caught sight of something behind her on a night-shelf over her bunk – a potted plant, almost identical with the one he had left on Kyril.

She saw the direction of his gaze. Her mouth came shut. She gasped, 'You know then!' It was almost a whisper. 'Kill me, destroy me, I am tired of life!'

She rose to her feet, arms out defenselessly. Joe arose, moved a step toward her. It was like a dream, a time past the edge of reason, without logic, cause, effect. Her eyes widened, not in fear now. He put his hands on her shoulders. She was warm and slender, pulsing like a bird.

She pulled away, sat back on her bed. 'I don't understand,' she said in a husky voice. 'I understand nothing.'

'Tell me,' said Joe in a voice almost as husky. 'What is this Manaolo to you? Is he your lover?'

She said nothing; then at last gave her head a little shake. 'No, he is nothing. He has been sent to Ballenkarch on a mission. I decided I wanted release from the rituals. I wanted adventure, and cared nothing for consequence. But Manaolo frightens me. He came to me yesterday – but I was afraid.'

Joe felt a wonderful yeastiness around his heart. The image of Margaret appeared, mouth puckered accusingly. Joe sighed regretfully. The mood changed. Elfane's face was once more that of a young Druid Priestess.

'What is your business, Smith?' she asked coolly. 'Are you a spy?'

'No, I'm not a spy.'

'Then why do you go to Ballenkarch? Only spies and agents go to Ballenkarch. Druids and Mangs or their hirelings.'

'It is business of a personal nature.' Looking at her he reflected that this vivid Priestess Elfane had gaily suggested killing him only yesterday.

She noticed his scrutiny, tilted her head in a whimsical harlequin grimace – the trick of a girl aware of her appeal, a flirtatious trick. Joe laughed – stopped, listened. There had been a scraping sound against the wall.

Elfane followed his gaze.

'That's my cabin!' Joe rose to his feet, opened the door, bounded down the balcony, threw open the door to his cabin. Erru Ex Amma, the young Mang officer, stood facing him, a wide mirthless grin on his face, showing pointed yellow teeth. He held a gun which was directed at Joe's middle.

'Back up!' he ordered. *'Back!'*

Joe slowly retreated out on the balcony. He looked over into the saloon. The four Mangs were at their game. One of the civilians glanced up, muttered to the others and they all turned their heads, looked up. Joe caught the flash of four citron-yellow faces. Then they were back to their game.

'Into the she-Druid's cabin,' said Ex Amma. *'Quick!'* He moved his gun, still smiling the wide smile that was like a fox showing its fangs.

Joe slowly backed into Elfane's cabin, eyes flicking back and forth between the gun and the Mang's face.

Elfane gasped, sighed in terror. The Mang saw the pot with the bit of plant sprouting from it. 'Ahhhh!'

He turned to Joe. 'Back against the wall.' He gave his gun a little forward motion, grimaced with anticipation and Joe knew he was about to die.

The door behind slid open; there was a hiss. The Mang stiffened, bent backward in an agonized arc, threw up his head, his jaw strained in a soundless scream. He fell to the deck.

Hableyat stood in the doorway, smiling primly. 'I'm very sorry that there should have been this disturbance.'

VI

Hableyat's eyes went to the plant on the shelf. He shook his head, clicked his tongue, turned a reproachful gaze on Joe. 'My dear fellow, you have been instrumental in ruining a very careful plan.'

'If you had asked me,' said Joe, 'if I wanted to donate my life to the success of your schemes I could have saved you a lot of grief.'

Hableyat bleated his laugh without moving a muscle of his face. 'You are charming. I am happy that you are still with us. But now I fear there is to be a quarrel.'

The three Mangs were marching in belligerent single-file along the balcony, the old officer, Erru Kametin, in the lead, followed by the two civilians. Erru Kametin came to a stiff halt, bristling like an angry cur. 'Lord Hableyat, this is sheer outrage. You have interfered with an officer of the Reach in his duty.'

' "Interfered"?' protested Hableyat. 'I have killed him. As to his "duty" – since when has a rakehelly Red-branch tag-at-heels been ranked with a member of the Ampianu General?'

'We have our orders direct from Magnerru Ippolito. You have no slightest supercession —'

'Magnerru Ippolito, if you recall,' said Hableyat smoothly, 'is responsible to the Lathbon, who sits with the Blue-water on the General.'

'A pack of white-blooded cravens!' shouted the officer. 'You and the rest of the Bluewaters!'

The Mang woman on the main deck, who had been straining to glimpse the events on the balcony, screamed.

Then came Manaolo's metallic voice. 'Miserable dingy dogs!'

He bounded up to the balcony, lithe and strong, tremendous in his fury. With one hand he seized the shoulder of one civilian, hurled him to the catwalk, did the same for the other. He lifted Erru Kametin, tossed him bodily over the balcony. Dropping slowly in the half-gravity Erru Kametin landed with a grunt. Manaolo turned to Hableyat, who held out a protesting hand.

'A moment, Ecclesiarch, please use no force on my poor corpulence.'

The wild face showed no flicker of emotion. The crouch of his body was answer to Hableyat's words.

Joe drew in his breath, stepped forward, threw a left jab, a hard right and Manaolo sprawled to the deck, where he lay looking at Joe with dead-black eyes.

'Sorry,' lied Joe. 'But Hableyat just saved my life and Elfane's. Give him time to talk anyway.'

Manaolo jumped to his feet, without a word entered Elfane's cabin, shut and locked the door. Hableyat turned, stared quizzically at Joe. 'We have returned each other compliments.'

Joe said, 'I'd like to know what's going on. No, I don't either – I want to mind my own business. I have my own troubles. I wish you'd keep yours to yourself.'

Hableyat shook his head slowly as if in puzzled admiration. 'For one of your professed intent you hurl yourself into the thick of things. But if you'll come to my cabin I have an excellent aquavit which will form the basis of a pleasant relaxation.'

'Poison?' inquired Joe.

Hableyat shook his head gravely. 'Merely excellent brandy.'

The captain of the vessel called a meeting of the passengers. He was a large heavy man with dead-white hair, a flat-white face, liquid-green eyes, a thin pink mouth. He wore the Beland skin-tight garment of dark-green with glass epaulets and a scarlet ruff above each elbow.

The passengers sat in the deep couches – the two civilian Mangs; the woman, red-eyed from crying, Erru Kametin, Hableyat, serene and easy in a loose robe of a dull white stuff with Joe next to him. Beside Joe sat the gaunt bald woman in the black gown and she had a sickly-sweet odor about her that was neither floral nor animal. Then came the Cils, then the two Druids, placid and secure, then Elfane and last, Manaolo. He wore a striking garment of light-green sateen with gold striping along the legs. A light flat morion perched jauntily on his dark curls.

The captain spoke ponderously. 'I am aware that a tension exists between the worlds of Kyril and Mangtse. But this ship is the property of Beland, and we are resolved to remain dispassionate and neutral.

'There was a killing this morning. So far as I have been able to gather Erru Ex Amma was discovered searching the cabin of Lord Smith and, when apprehended, forced Smith into the cabin of the Priestess Alnietho' – using the name Elfane had signed to the passenger list – 'where he threatened to kill them both. Lord Hableyat, in a praiseworthy effort to avoid an interplanetary incident, appeared and killed his countryman Erru Ex Amma.

'The other Mangs, protesting, were engaged violently by Ecclesiarch Manaolo, who also began to attack Lord Hableyat. Lord Smith, anxious lest Manaolo, in his ignorance of the true state of affairs, injure Lord Hableyat, struck Manaolo with his fist. I believe, in essence, that is the gist of the affair.'

He paused. No one spoke. Hableyat sat twiddling his

forefingers around each other with his plump lower lips hanging loose. Joe was aware of Elfane sitting stiff and silent and he felt a slow look from Manaolo drift over him – his face, shoulders, legs.

The captain continued. 'To the best of my belief, the culprit in this case, Erru Ex Amma, has been punished by death. The rest of you are guilty of nothing more than hot tempers. But I do not propose to countenance further incidents. On any such occasion the participants will be hypnotized and webbed into their hammocks for the duration of the voyage.

'It is Beland tradition that our ships are neutral ground and our livelihood stems from this reputation. I will not see it challenged. Quarrels, personal or inter-planetary, must wait till you are away from my authority.' He bowed heavily. 'Thank you for your attention.'

The Mangs immediately arose, the woman departing for her cabin to weep, the three men to their game with the colored bars, Hableyat to the promenade. The gaunt woman sat without movement, staring at the spot where the captain had stood. The Cils wandered to the ship's library. The Druid missionaries converged on Manaolo.

Elfane arose, stretched her slim young arms, looked quickly toward Joe, then to Manaolo's broad back. She made up her mind, crossed the room to Joe, settled on the couch beside him. 'Tell me, Lord Smith – what did Hableyat talk to you about when he took you to his room?'

Joe moved uneasily in his seat. 'Priestess – I can't be a tale-bearer between Druids and Mangs. In this particular case we spoke of nothing very important. He asked me about my life on Earth, he was interested in the man I've come out here seeking. I described a number of the planets I've stopped at. We drank a good deal of brandy, and that was about all there was to it.'

Elfane bit her lip impatiently. 'I cannot understand why Hableyat protected us from the young Mang... What does he gain? He is as completely Mang as the other. He would die rather than allow the Druids to take sovereignty over Ballenkarch.'

Joe said, 'You and Manaolo are certainly not en route to take over sovereignity of Ballenkarch?'

She gave him a wide-eyed stare, then drummed her fingers on her leg. Joe smiled to himself. In anyone else the assumptions of unlimited authority would be a matter of serious irritation. In Elfane – Joe, charmed and bewitched, dismissed it as an intriguing mannerism. He laughed.

'Why do you laugh?' she asked suspiciously.

'You remind me of a kitten dressed up in doll's clothes – very proud of itself.'

She flushed, her eyes sparkled. 'So – you laugh at me!'

After an instant of contemplation Joe asked, 'Don't you ever laugh at yourself?'

'No. Of course not.'

'Try it some time.' He arose to his feet, went to the gymnasium.

VII

Joe worked up a sweat in an obstacle treadmill, jumped out, sat panting on the bench. Manaolo came slowly into the gymnasium, looked up and down the floor, then slowly back to Joe. Joe thought, *Here comes trouble.*

Manaolo glanced back over his shoulder, then turned crossed the room in three strides. He stood looking down at Joe. His face was not a man's face but a glimpse into a fantasy of the underworld.

He said, 'You touched me with your hands.'

'Touched you, hell!' said Joe. 'I knocked you A over T.'

Manaolo's mouth, tender enough to be a woman's but also hard and muscular, sunk at the corners. He writhed his shoulders, leaned forward, kicked. Joe bent double in silent agony, clasping his lower abdomen. Manaolo stepped lightly back, kicked under Joe's jaw.

Joe slid slowly, laxly to the deck. Manaolo bent swiftly, a little metal device glittering in his hands. Joe raised his arm feebly – Manaolo kicked it aside. He hooked the metal instrument in Joe's nostrils, jerked. Two little hooked knives sliced the cartilage. A cloud of powder seared the flesh.

Manaolo jumped back, the corners of his mouth pushed in deeper. He turned on his heel, swung jauntily out of the room.

The ship's doctor said, 'There – it's not too bad. You'll have the two scars for awhile but they shouldn't be too noticeable.'

Joe examined his reflection in the mirror – his bruised chin, the plastered nose. 'Well – I've still got a nose.'

'You've still got a nose,' the doctor agreed woodenly. 'Lucky I got you in time. I've had some experience with that powder. It's a hormone promoting the growth of skin. If it hadn't been removed, the splits would be permanent and you'd have three flaps on your face.'

'You understand,' said Joe, 'this was an accident. I wouldn't want to trouble the captain with any report and I hope you won't.'

The doctor shrugged, turned, put away his equipment. 'Strange accident.'

Joe returned to the saloon. The Cils were learning the game with the colored bars, chatting gaily with the Mangs. The Druid missionaries, heads together, were performing some intricate ritual at their portable alter. Hableyat was spread comfortably on a couch, examining his fingernails with every evidence of satisfaction. The door from Elfane's cabin opened, Manaolo stepped out, swung easily along the balcony, down the steps. He gave Joe an expressionless glance, turned up toward the promenade.

Joe settled beside Hableyat, felt his nose tenderly. 'It's still there.'

Hableyat nodded composedly. 'It will be as good as new in a week or two. These Beland medics are apt, very apt. Now on Kyril, where doctors are nonexistent, the man of the Laity would apply a poultice of some vile material and the wound would never heal.

'You will notice a large number of the Laity with tri-cleft noses. Next to killing it is a favorite Druid punishment.' He surveyed Joe from under half-closed lids. 'You seem to be rather less exercised than would be permissible under the circumstances.'

'I'm not pleased.'

'Let me cite you a facet of Druid psychology,' said Hableyat. 'In Manaolo's mind the infliction of the wound terminated the matter. It was the final decisive act in the quarrel between you two. On Kyril the Druids act without fear of retaliation in the name of the Tree. It gives them a peculiar sense of infallibility. Now, I mention this merely to point out that Manaolo will be surprised and outraged if you pursue the matter further.'

Joe shrugged.

Hableyat said in a querulous voice, 'You say nothing, you make no threats, you voice no anger.'

Joe smiled a rather thin smile. 'I haven't had time for much but amazement. Give me time.'

Hableyat nodded.

'Ah, I see. You were shocked by the attack.'

'Very much so.'

Hableyat nodded again, a series of wise little jerks that set his dewlaps quivering. 'Let us change the subject then. Now your description of the European pre-Christian Druids interests me.'

'Tell me something,' said Joe. 'What is that pot that all the fuss is about? Some kind of message or formula or military secret?'

Hableyat's eyes widened. 'Message? Military secret? What *are* these? No, my dear fellow, to the best of my knowledge the pot is merely an honest pot and the plant an honest plant.'

'Why the excitement then? And why try to stick me with a ringer?'

Hableyat said musingly, 'Sometimes in affairs of planetary scope it becomes necessary to sacrifice the convenience of one person for the eventual benefit of many. You were to carry the plant to decoy my pistol-flourishing compatriots from that conveyed by the Druids.'

'I don't get it,' said Joe. 'Aren't you both working for

the same government?'

'Oh indeed,' said Hableyat. 'Our aims are identical – the glorification and prosperity of our beloved planet. No one is more dedicated than myself. But there is a rather odd cleavage in the Mang system, separating the Red-branch Militars from the Bluewater Commercials. They exist like two souls in one body, two husbands married to the same wife.

'Both love Mangtse. Both use their peculiar means for displaying this love. To some extent they cooperate but only as is expedient. They are ultimately responsible only to the Lathbon and, a step lower, to the Ampianu General, in which body both seat members. In many ways the arrangement works well – sometimes two approaches to a problem are valuable.

'In general the Redbranch is direct and forceful. They believe that the best way to end our difficulties with the Druids is to seize the planet in a military operation. We Bluewaters point out that many men would be killed, much material destroyed and, if by some miracle we finally overcame the religion-crazed hordes of the Laity, we would have destroyed whatever usefulness Kyril might have for us.

'You see,' he nodded wisely at Joe, 'with a productive peasantry Kyril can produce the raw materials and handcrafts for our Mang industries. We form a natural couple but the current Druid policy is a disturbing factor. An industrialized Ballenkarch ruled by the Druids would upset the balance. Now the Redbranches want to destroy the Druids. We Bluewaters hope to influence a gradual metamorphosis toward an economy on Kyril channeled into production instead of into the Tree.'

'And how do you propose to work that out?'

Hableyat wagged a solemn finger. 'In the strictest confidence, my dear fellow – by letting the Druids proceed undisturbed with their intrigues.'

Joe frowned, touched his nose absently. 'But – this flowerpot – how does it enter the picture?'

'That,' said Hableyat, 'is what the poor single-minded Druids conceive to be the most cogent instrument of their plan. I hope it will be one of the instruments of their defeat. So I mean to see that the pot reaches Ballenkarch if I must kill twenty of my fellow Mangs in the process.'

'If you're telling the truth, which I doubt —'

'But my dear fellow, why should I lie to you?'

'— I commence to understand some of this madhouse.'

Junction – a many-sided polyhedron one mile in diameter, swimming in a diffused luminescence. A dozen spaceships suckled up close like leeches and nearby space was thick with firefly flecks of light – men and women in airsuits, drifting through the void, venturing off ten, twenty, thirty miles, feeling the majesty of deep space.

There seemed to be no formalities connected with landing – a matter which surprised Joe, who had become accustomed to elaborate checking and rechecking, indexes, reserve numbers, inspections, quarantine, passes, visas, reviews, signatures and countersignatures. The *Belsaurion* nosed up to a vacant port, clamped itself to the seal with mesonic glue-fields and so came to rest.

The hypnots in the hold lay undisturbed.

The Beland captain once again called a meeting of the passengers. 'We are now at Junction, and will remain thirty-two hours while we take on mail and freight. Now some of you have been here before. I need not caution you to discretion.

'For those who visit Junction for the first time I will state that it lies in no planet's jurisdiction, that its law is at the whim of the owner and his comptroller, that their

71

main interest is in extracting money from your pockets through pleasures and pastimes of various natures.

'Thus I urge you, beware of the gambling cages. I say to you women – do not enter the Perfume Park alone for that is a signal that you wish a paid escort. The men who patronize Tier Three will find it expensive and perhaps dangerous. There have been cases of murder for robbery reported. A man engrossed with a girl is an easy target for a knife. Again films have been made of persons engaged in questionable acts, and these have been used for blackmail.

'Lastly let no desire for excitement or thrill take you down to the Arena – because you may easily be forced into the ring and set to fighting an expert warrior. Once you pay admission you put yourself at the choice of whoever is victor at the moment. It is astonishing how many casual visitors, whether under the influence of drugs, alcohol, lust for excitement or sheer bravado, dare the Arena. A good number of them are killed or seriously injured.

'Enough for the warnings. I do not wish to alarm you. There are a number of legitimate pleasures you may indulge in. The Nineteen Gardens are the talk of the Universe. In the Celestium you may dine on food of your planet, hear your native music. The shops along the Esplanade sell anything you may desire at very reasonable prices.

'So with this warning I put you on your own. Thirty-two hours from now we leave for Ballenkarch.'

He withdrew. There was a general shuffling of feet. Joe noticed that Manaolo followed Elfane to her cabin. The two Druid missionaries returned to their portable alter, apparently with no intention of going ashore. The Mang officer, Erru Kametin, marched off with the young widow at his heels and after them went the two Mangs in civilian dress.

The gaunt bald old woman moved not an inch from her chair but sat staring across the floor. The Cils, giggling, stepping high, rushed from the ship. Hableyat stopped before Joe, plump arms clasped behind his back. 'Well, my friend, are you going ashore?'

'Yes,' said Joe. 'I think I probably will. I'm waiting to see what the Priestess and Manaolo will do.'

Hableyat teetered on his heels. 'Steer clear of that chap is my best advice. He's a vicious example of megalomania – conditioned, I may add, to its most exquisite pitch by his environment. Manaolo considers himself divine and ordained – actually, literally – to a degree neither of us can imagine. Manaolo knows no right or wrong. He knows pro and con Manaolo.'

The door to Cabin 13 opened. Manaolo and Elfane stepped out on the balcony. Manaolo, in the lead, carried a small parcel. He wore a chased cuirass of gold and bright metal and a long green cloak, embroidered with yellow leaves, was flung back from his shoulders. Looking to neither right nor left he strode down the stairs, across the cabin, out the port.

Elfane halted on reaching the saloon deck, looked after him, shook her head – a motion eloquent of annoyance. She turned, crossed the saloon to Joe and Hableyat.

Hableyat made a respectful inclination of the head, which Elfane acknowledged coolly. She said to Joe, 'I want you to conduct me ashore.'

'Is that an invitation or an order?'

Elfane raised her eyebrows quizzically. 'It means I want you to take me ashore.'

'Very well,' said Joe, rising to his feet. 'I'll be glad to.'

Hableyat sighed. 'If only I were young and handsome —'

73

Joe snorted. 'Handsome?'

'— no lovely young lady would need to ask me twice.'

Elfane said in a tight voice, 'I think it's only fair to mention that Manaolo promised to kill you if he finds you talking to me.'

There was silence. Then Joe said in a voice that sounded strange in his own ears, 'So the very first thing, you come over and ask me to take you ashore.'

'Are you frightened?'

'I'm not brave.'

She turned sharply, started for the port. Hableyat said curiously, 'Why did you do that?'

Joe snorted angrily. 'She's a troublemaker. She has a ridiculous notion that I'll risk some crazy Druid shooting me down like a dog merely for the privilege of walking her around.' He watched her leave the ship, slim as a birch in her dark blue cape. 'She's right,' said Joe. 'I *am* just that kind of damn fool.'

He started off after her on the run. Hableyat watched them go off together, smiled sadly, rubbed his hands together. Then unbuckling the robe from around his paunch, he sat back on the couch once again, dreamily followed the devotions of the two Druids at their altar.

VIII

They were walking down a corridor lined with small shops. 'Look,' said Joe, 'are you a Druid Priestess, about as likely to lop the life out of a commoner as not – or are you a nice kid out on a date?'

Elfane tossed her head, tried to look dignified and worldly. 'I am a very important person and one day I will be the Suppliant for the entire Shire of Kelminester. A small shire, true, but the guidance of three million souls to the Tree will be in my hands.'

Joe gave her a disgusted look. 'Won't they do just as well without you?'

She laughed, relaxed for an instant to become a gay dark-haired girl. 'Oh – probably. But I'm forced to keep up appearances.'

'The trouble is that after awhile you'll start believing all that stuff.'

She said nothing for a moment. Then, mischievously, 'Why are you looking about so attentively? Is this corridor so interesting then?'

'I'm watching for that devil Manaolo,' said Joe. 'It would be just like him to be lurking in one of these shadows and step out and stab me.'

Elfane shook her head. 'Manaolo has gone down to Tier Three. He has tried to make me his lover every night of the voyage but I have no desire for him. This morning he threatened that unless I yielded he would debauch himself along the Tier. I told him by all means to do so and then perhaps his virility would not be so ardently directed against me. He left in a huff.'

'Manaolo always seems to be in a state of offended dignity.'

'He is a man with a very exalted rank,' said Elfane. 'Now let us go down here. I wish to —'

Joe took her arm, swung her around, gazed into her startled eyes, her nose an inch from his.

'Look here, young lady. I'm not trying to assert my virility but I'm not trotting here and there after you, carrying your bundles like a chauffeur.'

He knew it was the wrong word.

'Chauffeur, *ha*! Then —'

'If you don't like my company.' said Joe, 'now's the time to leave.'

After a moment she said, 'What's your name beside Smith?'

'Call me Joe.'

'Joe — you're a very remarkable man. Very strange. You puzzle me, Joe.'

'If you want to come with me — a chauffeur, a mechanic, a civil engineer, a moss-planter, a bartender, a tennis instructor, a freight docker, a dozen other things — we're going down to the Nineteen Gardens and see if they sell Earth-style beer.'

The Nineteen Gardens occupied a slice through the middle of the construction — nineteen wedge-shaped sections surrounding a central platform which served as a restaurant.

They found a vacant table and, to Joe's surprise, beer in frosted quart beakers was set before them without comment.

'If it pleases your Divinity,' said Elfane meekly.

Joe grinned sheepishly. 'You don't need to carry it that far. It must be a Druid trait, an avalanche one way, another way, all the way. Well, what did you want?'

'Nothing.' She turned in her seat, looked out across

76

the gardens. At this point Joe realized that willy-nilly, for good or bad, he was wildly enamored. Margaret? He sighed. She was far away, a thousand light-years.

He looked across the gardens, nineteen of them, flora of nineteen different planets, each with its distinctive color timbres – black, gray and white of Kelce – oranges, yellows, hot lime green of Zarjus – the soft pastel pink, green, blue and yellow blossoms which grew on the quiet little planets of Jonapah – green in a hundred rich tones, gay red, sky blue – Joe started, half-rose to his feet.

'What's the matter?' asked Elfane.

'That garden there – those are Earth plants or I'm a ring-tailed monkey.' He jumped up, went to the rail and she followed. 'Geraniums, honeysuckle, petunias, zinnia, roses, Italian cypress, poplars, weeping willows. And a lawn. And hibiscus . . .' He looked at the descriptive plaque. 'Planet Gea. Location uncertain.'

They returned to the table. 'You act as if you're homesick,' said Elfane in an injured voice.

Joe smiled. 'I am – very homesick. Tell me something about Ballenkarch.'

She tasted the beer, looked at it in surprise, screwed up her face.

'Nobody likes beer when they first drink it,' said Joe.

'Well – I don't know too much about Ballenkarch. Up to a few years ago it was completely savage. No ships stopped there because the autochthones were cannibals. Then the present prince united all of the smaller continent into a nation. It happened overnight. Many people were killed.

'But now there is no more murder and ships can land in comparative safety. The Prince has decided to industrialize and he's imported much machinery from Beland, Mangtse and Grabo across the stream. Little by little he's extending his rule over the main continent –

77

winning over the chiefs, hypnotizing them or killing them.

'Now you must understand the Ballenkarts have no religion whatever and we Druids hope to tie their new industrial power to us through the medium of a common faith. Then we will no longer depend on Mangtse for manufactured goods. The Mangs naturally don't care for the idea and so they are . . .' Her eyes widened. She reached across, grasped his arm. 'Manaolo! Oh Joe, I hope he doesn't see us.'

Joe's mantle of caution ripped. Humility is impossible when the object of your love is fearing for your safety.

He sat back in his seat, watched Manaolo come striding onto the terrace like a Demonland hero. A beige-skinned woman, wearing orange pantaloons, pointed slippers of blue cloth and a blue cloth cap, hung on his arm. In his other arm he carried the parcel he had taken off the ship. In the flicker of his dead eyes he saw Elfane and Joe, changed his course without expression, sauntered across the floor, casually drawing a stiletto from his belt.

'This is it,' muttered Joe. 'This is it!' He rose to his feet.

Diners, drinkers, scattered. Manaolo stopped a yard distant, the ghost of a smile on his dark face. He set the parcel on the table, then easily stepped forward, thrust. It was done with an almost naïve simplicity as if he expected Joe to stand still to be stabbed. Joe threw the beer into his face, hit his wrist with the beaker and the stiletto tinkled to the ground.

'Now,' said Joe, 'I'm going to beat you within an inch of your life.'

Manaolo lay on the ground. Joe, panting, straddled him. The bandage across his nose had broken. Blood flowed down his face, down his chin. Manaolo's hand fell

78

on the stiletto. With a subdued grunt he swung. Joe gripped the arm, guided it past him into Manaolo's shoulder.

Manaolo grunted once more, plucked the blade loose. Joe seized it away, stuck it through Manaolo's ear into the wooden floor, pounded it deep with blows of his fist, jumped to his feet, stood looking down.

Manaolo flopped like a fish, lay still, exhausted. An impassive litter crew came through the crowd, removed the stiletto, loaded him on the litter, bore him away. The beige-skinned woman ran along beside him. Manaolo spoke to her. She turned, ran to the table, took the parcel, ran back to where the attendants were loading Manaolo into a wheeled vehicle, placed the parcel on his chest.

Joe sank back into his chair, took Elfane's beer, drank deeply.

'Joe,' she whispered. 'Are you – hurt?'

'I'm black and blue all over,' said Joe. 'Manaolo's a rough boy. If you hadn't been here I would have ducked him. But,' he said with a blood-smeared grin, 'I couldn't let you see me ducking my rival.'

'Rival?' she looked puzzled. 'Rival?'

'For you.'

'Oh!' in a colorless tone.

'Now don't say "I'm the Royal Druid God-almighty Priestess"!'

She looked up startled. 'I wasn't thinking of that. I was thinking that Manaolo never was – your rival.'

Joe said, 'I've got to clean up and get some new clothes. Would you like to come with me or —'

'No,' said Elfane, still in the colorless voice. 'I'll stay here awhile. I want to – to think.'

Thirty-one hours. The *Belsaurion* was due to take off.

The passengers trickled back on board to be checked in by the purser.

Thirty-one and a half hours. 'Where's Manaolo?' Elfane asked the purser. 'Has he come aboard?'

'No, Worship.'

Elfane chewed her lip, clenched her hands. 'I'd better check at the hospital. You won't go off without me?'

'No, Worship, certainly not.'

Joe followed her to a telephone. 'Hospital,' she said to the mechanical voice. Then, 'I want to inquire about Ecclesiarch Manaolo, who was brought in yesterday. Has he been discharged? . . . Very well but hurry. His ship is waiting to take off . . .' She turned a side comment to Joe. 'They've gone to check at his room.'

A moment passed; then she bent to the ear-phone. '*What!* No!'

'What's the trouble?'

'He's dead. He's been murdered.'

The captain agreed to hold the ship until Elfane returned from the hospital. She ran to the elevator with Joe at her heels. In the hospital she was led to a lank Beland nurse with white hair wound into a severe bun.

'Are you his wife?' asked the nurse. 'If so will you please make the arrangements for the body.'

'I'm not his wife. I don't care what you do with the body. Tell me, what became of the parcel he brought in here with him?'

'There's no parcel in his room. I remember he brought one in with him – but it's not there now.'

Joe asked, 'What visitors did he have?'

'I'm not sure. I could find out, I suppose.'

Manaolo's last visitors were three Mangs, who had signed unfamiliar names to the register. The corridor attendant had noticed that one of them, an elderly man with a rigid military posture, had emerged from the room carrying a parcel.

Elfane leaned against Joe's shoulder. 'That was the pot with the plant in it.' He put his arms around her, patted her dark head. 'And now the Mangs have it,' she said hopelessly.

'Excuse me if I'm excessively curious,' said Joe. 'But what is there in that pot which makes it so important?'

She looked at him tearfully, finally said, 'The second most important living thing in the universe. The only living shoot from the Tree of Life.'

They slowly returned along the blue-tiled corridor toward the ship. Joe said, 'I'm not only curious but I'm stupid as well. Why bother to carry a shoot from the Tree of Life all over creation? Unless, of course —'

She nodded. 'As I told you we wished to form a bond with the Ballenkarts — a religious bond. This shoot, the Son of the Tree, would be the vital symbol.'

'Then,' said Joe, 'the Druids would gradually infiltrate, gradually dominate, until Ballenkarch was another Kyril. Five billion miserable serfs, a million or two high-living Druids, one Tree.' He examined her critically. 'Aren't there any on Kyril who consider the system — well, unbalanced?'

She burnt him with an indignant look. 'You're a complete Materialist. On Kyril Materialism is an offense punishable by death.'

' "Materialism" meaning "distribution of the profits," ' suggested Joe, 'Or maybe "incitement to rebellion." '

'Life is a threshold to glory,' said Elfane. 'Life is the effort which determines one's place on the Tree. The industrious workers become leaves high in the Scintillance. The sluggard must grope forever through dark slime as a rootlet.'

'If Materialism is the sin you seem to believe it is — why do the Druids eat so high off the hog? Which means, live in such pampered luxury? Doesn't it seem strange to you that those who stand to lose the most by "Materialism" are those most opposed to it?'

'Who are you to criticize?,' she cried angrily. 'A barbarian as savage as the Ballenkarts! If you were on Kyril your wild talk would quickly be shut off!'

'Still the tin goddess, aren't you?' said Joe contemptuously.

In outraged silence she stalked ahead. Joe grinned to himself, followed her back to the ship.

The lock into the ship opened. Elfane stopped short. 'The Son is lost – probably destroyed.' She looked sidewise at Joe. 'There is no reason why I should continue to Ballenkarch. My duty is to return home, report to the College of Thearchs.'

Joe rubbed his chin ruefully. He had been hoping that this aspect to the matter would not occur to her. He said tentatively, not quite sure how much anger she felt toward him, 'But you left Kyril with Manaolo to escape the life of the palace. The Thearchs will learn every detail of Manaolo's death through their spies.'

She inspected him with an expression unreadable to his Earthly perceptions. 'You want me to continue with you?'

'Yes, I do.'

'Why?'

'I'm afraid,' said Joe with a sad droop to his mouth, 'that you affect me very intensely, very pleasantly. This in spite of your warped philosophy.'

'That was the right answer,' announced Elfane. 'Very well, I will continue. Perhaps,' she said importantly, 'perhaps I'll be able to persuade the Ballenkarts to worship the Tree on Kyril.'

Joe held his breath for fear of laughing and so offending her once more. She looked at him somberly. 'I realize you find me amusing.'

Hableyat stood by the purser's desk. 'Ah – back, I see. And Manaolo's assassins have escaped with the Son of the Tree?'

Elfane froze in her tracks. 'How did you know?'

'My dear Priestess,' said Hableyat, 'the smallest pebble dropped in the pond sends its ripples to the far shore. Indeed, I see that I am perhaps even closer to the true state of affairs than you are.'

'What do you mean by that?'

The port clanged, the steward politely said, 'We take off in ten minutes. Priestess, my Lords, may I web you into your berths against the climb into speed?'

IX

Joe awoke from his trance. Remembering the last awakening he jerked up in his web, searched the cabin. But he was alone and the door was locked, bolted, barred as he had arranged it before taking the pill and turning hypnotic patterns on the screen.

Joe jumped out of the hammock, bathed, shaved, climbed into the new suit of blue gabardine he had bought at Junction. Stepping out on the balcony, he found the saloon almost dark. Evidently he had awakened early.

He stopped by the door to Cabin 13, thought of Elfane lying warm and limp within, her dark hair tumbled on the pillow, her face, smoothed of doubts and prideful mannerisms. He put his hand to the door. It was as if something dragged it there. By an effort of will he pulled the arm back, turned, moved along the balcony. He stopped short. Someone sat in the big lounge by the observation port. Joe leaned forward, squinted into the gloom. Hableyat.

Joe continued along the balcony, down the steps. Hableyat made a courtly gesture of greeting. 'Sit down, my friend, and join me in my pre-prandial contemplations.'

Joe took a seat. 'You awoke early.'

'To the contrary,' said Hableyat. 'I did not submit to slumber. I have been sitting here in this lounge six hours and you are the first person I have seen.'

'Whom were you expecting?'

Hableyat allowed a wise expression to form on his

yellow face. 'I expected no one *in particular*. But from a few adroit questions and interviews at the Junction I find that people are not all they seem. I was curious to observe any activity in the light of this new knowledge.'

Joe said with a sigh, 'After all, it's none of *my* business.'

Hableyat waggled his plump forefinger. 'No, no, my friend. You are modest. You dissemble. I fear that you have become very much engrossed in the fortunes of the lovely young Priestess and so cannot be considered dispassionate.'

'Put it this way. I don't care whether or not the Druids get their plant life to Ballenkarch. And I don't quite understand why you are so cooperative toward their efforts.' He glanced at Hableyat appraisingly. 'If I were the Druids I'd reconsider the whole idea.'

'Ah, my dear fellow,' beamed Hableyat, 'you compliment me. But I work in the dark. I grope. There are subtleties I have not yet fathomed. It would surprise you to learn the duplicity of some of our acquaintances.'

'Well, I'm willing to be surprised.'

'For instance – that bald old woman in the black dress, who sits and stares into space like one already dead, what do you think of her?'

'Oh – harmless unprepossessing old buzzard.'

'She is four hundred and twelve years old. Her husband, according to my informant, evolved an elixir of life when she was fourteen. She murdered him and only twenty years ago did she lose the freshness of her youth. During this time she has had lovers numbered by the thousands, of all shapes, sizes, sexes, races, bloods and colors. For the last hundred years her diet has consisted almost entirely of human blood.'

Joe sank into the seat, rubbed his face. 'Go on.'

'I learn that one of my countrymen is a great deal

higher in rank and authority than I had assumed, and that I must tread warily indeed. I find that the Prince of Ballenkarch has an agent aboard the ship.'

'Continue,' said Joe.

'I learned also — as perhaps I hinted before the take-off from Junction — that Manaolo's death and the loss of his flowerpot was perhaps not an unrelieved tragedy from the Druid standpoint.'

'How so?'

Hableyat looked thoughtfully up along the balcony. 'Has it ever occurred to you,' he asked slowly, 'that Manaolo was an odd choice for courier on a mission of such importance?'

Joe frowned. 'I rather imagined that he fell into the commission through his rank — which, according to El-fane, is — was — rather exalted. An Ecclesiarch, right under a Thearch.'

'But the Druids are not completely inflexible and stupid,' said Hableyat patiently. 'They have managed to control five billion men and women with nothing more than a monstrous tree for almost a thousand years. They are not dolts.

'The College of Thearchs no doubt knew Manaolo for what he was — a swaggering egocentric. They decided that he would make the ideal stalking-horse. I, not understanding the intricacy of the plan, decided that Manaolo in turn needed a decoy to divert attention from him. For this purpose I selected you.

'But the Druids had foreseen the difficulty in the mission, and had made arrangements. Manaolo was sent out with a spurious seedling with exactly the right degree of ostentatious stealth. The real Son of the Tree was conveyed in another manner.'

'And this other manner?'

Hableyat shrugged. 'I can only theorize. Perhaps the Priestess has it cunningly concealed about her person. Perhaps the shoot has been entrusted to the baggage car – though this I doubt through fear of our spies. I imagine the shoot is in the custody of some representative of Kyril. . . . Perhaps on this ship, perhaps on another.'

'And so?'

'And so I sit here and watch to see if anyone shares my suspicion. So far you are the first to appear.'

Joe smiled faintly. 'And what conclusions do you draw?'

'None.'

The white-haired steward appeared, his legs and arms thin and peculiarly graceful in the skin-tight cloth. Cloth? Joe, for the first time, looked closely. The steward asked, 'Will you gentlemen take breakfast?'

Hableyat nodded. 'I will.'

Joe said, 'I'll have some fruit.' Then emboldened by his discovery of beer at Junction, 'I don't suppose you have coffee.'

'I think we can find some, Lord Smith.'

Joe turned to Hableyat. 'They don't wear many clothes. That's *paint* on them!'

Hableyat appeared to be amused. 'Of course. Haven't you always known that the Belands wore more paint than clothes?'

'No,' said Joe. 'Clothes I've always taken for granted.'

'That's a grave mistake,' said Hableyat pompously. 'When you're dealing with any creature or manifestation or personality on a strange planet – *never take anything for granted!* When I was young I visited the world Xenchoy on the Kim and there I made the mistake of seducing one of the native girls. A delicious creature with vines plaited into her hair. I remember that she submitted readily but without enthusiasm.

'In my most helpless moment she attempted to stab me with a long knife. I protested and she was dumbfounded. Subsequently I found that on Xenchoy only a person intending suicide will possess a girl out of wedlock and since there is no onus either on suicide or impudicity he so achieves humanity's dream, of dying in ecstasy.'

'And the moral?'

'It is certainly clear. Things are not always what they seem.'

Joe relaxed into the couch, musing, while Hableyat hummed a four-toned Mang fugue under his breath, accompanying himself on six tablets hanging around his neck like a pendant, each of which vibrated to a different note when touched.

Joe thought, *It's evident he either knows or suspects something, which is plain as my face and I can't see it. Hableyat once said I have a limited intellect, maybe he's right. He's certainly given me enough hints. Elfane? Hableyat himself? No, he was talking about the Son of the Tree. A tremendous lot of excitement for a vegetable. Hableyat thinks its still aboard, that's clear. Well, I haven't got it. He doesn't have it or he wouldn't talk so much. Elfane is in the dark. The Cils? The horrible old woman? The Mangs? The two Druid missionaries?*

Hableyat was observing him closely. As Joe sat up with a jerk Hableyat smiled. 'Now do you understand?'

Joe said, 'It seems reasonable.'

The rating of passengers once more sat in the saloon but there was a different atmosphere now. The first leg of the voyage had suffered from tenseness but it had been a loose unpleasantness, a matter of personal likes and dislikes, dominated perhaps by the personality of Manaolo.

Now the individual relationships seemed submerged in more sweeping racial hatreds. Erru Kametin, the two Mang civilians – proctors of the Redbranch policy committee, so Joe learned from Hableyat – and the young Mang widow sat by the hour, playing their game with the colored bars, darting hot glances across the room at the imperturbable Hableyat.

The two Druid missionaries huddled over their altar in a dark corner of the saloon, busy with interminable rites before the representation of the Tree. The Cils, injured by the lack of response to their silken gambolings, kept to the promenade. The black-gowned woman sat still as death, her eyes moving an eighth of an inch from time to time. Perhaps once an hour she lifted a transparent hand up to her glass-bald pate.

Joe found himself buffeted by psychological crosscurrents, like a pond thrashed by winds from every direction at once. First there was his own mission to Ballenkarch. Strange, thought Joe – only days, hours to Ballenkarch and now his errand seemed drained of all urgency. He had only a given limited amount of emotion, of will, of power, and he seemed to have invested a large part of it in Elfane. Invested? It had been torn out of him, squeezed, wrenched.

Joe thought of Kyril, of the Tree. The palaces at Divinal clustered around the sub-planetary bulk of the trunk, the endless reaches of meager farms and ill-smelling villages, the slack-shouldered dead-eyed pilgrimage into the trunk, with the last triumphant gesture, the backward look off over the flat gray landscape.

He thought of Druid discipline – death. Though death was nothing to be feared on Kyril. Death was as common as eating. The Druid solution to any quandary – the avalanche – the all-the-way approach to existence. Moderation was a word with little meaning to men and women with no curb to any whim, indulgence or excess.

He considered what he knew of Mangtse – a small world of lakes and landscaped islands, a people with a love of intricate convolution, with an architecture of fanciful curves, looping wooden bridges over the streams and canals, charming picturesque vistas in the antique yellow light of the dim little sun.

Then the factories – neat, efficient, systematic, on the industrial islands. And the Mangs – a people as ornate, involute and subtle as their carved bridges. There was Hableyat, into whose soul Joe had seen for never an instant. There were the fire-breathing Redbranches bent on imperialism. In Earth terms – medievalists.

And Ballenkarch? Nothing except that it was a barbaric world with a prince intent on bringing an industrial complex into existence overnight. And somewhere on the planet, among the savages of the south or the barbarians of the north, was Harry Creath.

Harry had captured Margaret's imagination and taken light-hearted leave, leaving behind an emotional turmoil which could not be settled till Harry returned. Two years ago Harry had been only hours away on Mars. But when Joe arrived to bring him back to Earth for a showdown, Harry had left. Fuming at the delay, but tenacious and full of his obsession, Joe had persisted.

On Thuban he had lost the trail when a drunk's cutlass sent him to the hospital for three months. Then further months of agonized search and inquiry and at last the name of an obscure planet came to the surface – Ballenkarch. Then further months of working his way across the intervening galaxy. Now Ballenkarch lay ahead and somewhere on the planet was Harry Creath.

And Joe thought, *To hell with Harry!* Beacuse Margaret was no longer at the focus of his mind. Now it was an unprincipled minx of a Priestess. Joe pictured himself and Elfane exploring Earth's ancient playgrounds – Paris, Vienna, San Francisco, the Vale of Kashmir, the Black Forest, the Sahara Sea.

Then he asked himself, would Elfane *fit?* There were no dazed drudges on Earth to be killed or beaten or pampered like animals. Maybe there was Hableyat's meaning – *Things are not always what they seem.* Elfane appeared – fundamentally – a creature of his own general pattern. Perhaps he had never quite understood the profundity of Druid egotism. Very well then, he'd find out.

Hableyat looked up blandly as Joe got to his feet. 'If I were you, my friend, I think I would wait. At least another day. I doubt if as yet she has completely appreciated her own loneliness. I think that your appearance now, especially with that belligerent scowl on your face, would merely arouse her antagonism and she would class you with the rest of her enemies. Let her stew a day or so longer and then let her come upon you in the promenade – or the gymnasium, where I observe she spends an hour every day.'

Joe sank back on the couch. He said, 'Hableyat, you mystify me.'

Hableyat shook his head sadly. 'Ah, but I am transparent.'

'First on Kyril, you save my life. Then you try to get me killed.'

'Only as a disagreeable necessity.'

'At times I think you're friendly, sympathetic —'

'But of course!'

'— just as now you read my mind and give me fatherly advice. But – I'm never quite sure just what you're saving me for. Just as the goose being fattened for *paté de fois gras* never understands the unstinting generosity of his master. Things aren't always what they seem.' He laughed shortly. 'I don't suppose you'll tell me what slaughter you're fattening me for?'

Hableyat performed a gesture of polite confusion. 'Actually I am not at all devious. I make no pretenses, screen myself with nothing but honesty. My regard for you is genuine – but, I agree, that regard does not prevent me from sacrificing you for a greater end. There is no contradiction. I separate my personal tastes and aversions from my work. And so you know all about me.'

'How do I know when you're working and when you're not?'

Hableyat threw out his hands. 'It is a question not even I can answer.'

But Joe was not entirely dissatisfied. He sat back in the couch and Hableyat relaxed the band around his plump midriff.

'Life is very difficult at times,' said Hableyat, 'and very improbable, very taxing.'

'Hableyat,' said Joe, 'why don't you come back with me to Earth?'

Hableyat smiled. 'I may well heed your suggestion – if the Redbranches defeat the Bluewaters in the Ampianu.'

X

Four days out from Junction, three days to Ballenkarch. Joe, leaning at the rail in the belly of the ship's promenade, heard a slow step along the composition. It was Elfane. Her face was pale and haunted, her eyes were large and bright. She stopped hesitantly beside Joe as if she were only pausing in her walk.

Joe said, 'Hello,' and looked back to the stars.

By some subtlety of pose Elfane gave him to understand that she had definitely stopped, that she had joined him. She said, 'You've been avoiding me – when I need someone to talk to the most.'

Joe said searchingly, 'Elfane – have you ever been in love?'

Her face was puzzled. 'I don't understand.'

Joe grunted. 'Just an Earth abstraction. Whom do you mate with on Kyril?'

'Oh – persons who interest us, whom we like to be with, who make us conscious of our bodies.'

Joe turned back to the stars. 'The subject is a little deep.'

Her voice was amused and soft. 'I understand very well, Joe.'

He turned his head. She was smiling. Rich ripe lips, the passionate face, dark eyes holding an eagerness. He kissed her like a thirsty man drinking.

'Elfane . . . ?'

'Yes?'

'On Ballenkarch – we'll turn around, head back for Earth. No more worry, no more plotting, no more death.

There's so many places I want to show you – old places, old Earth, that's still so fresh and sweet.'

She moved in his arms. 'There's my own world, Joe – and my responsibility.'

Tensely Joe said, 'On Earth you'll see it as it is – a vile muck, as degrading to the Druids as it is miserable to the slaves.'

'Slaves? They serve the Tree of Life. We all serve the Tree of Life in our different ways.'

'The Tree of Death!'

Elfane disengaged herself without heat. 'Joe – it's something which I can't explain to you. We're bound to the Tree. We are its children. You don't understand the great truth. There is one universe, with the Tree at the hub, and the Druids and the Laity serve the Tree, at bay to pagan space.

'Someday it will be different. All men will serve the Tree. We'll be born from the soil, we'll serve and work and finally give our lives into the Tree and become a leaf in the eternal light, each to his place. Kyril will be the goal, the holy place of the galaxy.'

Joe protested, 'But you give this vegetable – an enormous vegetable but still a vegetable – you give this vegetable a higher place in your mind than you do humanity. On Earth we'd chop the thing up for stove wood. No, that's not true. We'd run a spiral runway around the thing, send excursion trips up and sell hot dogs and soda pop on the top. We'd use the thing, not let it hypnotize us by its bulk.'

She had not heard him. 'Joe – you can be my lover. And we'll live our life on Kyril and serve the Tree and kill its enemies . . .' She stopped short, stunned by Joe's expression.

'That's no good – for either of us. I'll go back to Earth. You stay out here, find another lover to kill your enemies for you. And we'll each be doing what we want. But the other won't be included.'

She turned away, leaned on the rail, stared dismally out at the midship stars. Presently, 'Were you ever in love with any other woman?'

'Nothing serious,' lied Joe. And, after a moment, 'And you – have you had other lovers?'

'Nothing serious . . .'

Joe looked at her sharply but there was no trace of humor on her face. He sighed. Earth was not Kyril.

She said, 'After we land on Ballenkarch what will you do?'

'I don't know – I haven't made up my mind. Certainly nothing to do with Druids and Mangs, I know that much. Trees and empires can all explode together so far as I'm concerned. I have problems of my own . . .' His voice dwindled, died.

He saw himself meeting Harry Creath. On Mars, with his mind full of Margaret – on Io, Pluto, Altair, Vega, Giansar, Polaris, Thuban, even as recently as Jamivetta and Kyril – he had been conscious of nothing quixotic, nothing ridiculous in his voyaging.

Now Margaret's image had begun to blur – but blurred as it was he heard the tinkling chime of her laugh. With a sudden flush of embarrassment he knew that she would find a great deal of amusement in the tale of his venturings – as well as astonishment, incredulity and perhaps the faintest hint of scorn.

Elfane was regarding him curiously. He came back to the present. Strange, how solid and real she seemed in contrast to his thought-waifs. Elfane would find nothing amusing in a man roaming the universe for love of her. On the contrary she would be indignant if such were not the case.

'What will you do on Ballenkarch then?' she asked.

Joe rubbed his chin, stared out at the shifting stars. 'I guess I'll look up Harry Creath.'

'And where will you look for him?'

'I don't know. I'll try the civilized continent first.'

'None of Ballenkarch is civilized.'

'The least barbarian continent, then!' said Joe patiently. 'If I know Harry, he'll be in the thick of things.'

'And if he's dead?'

'Then I'll turn around and go home with my conscience clear.'

Margaret would say, 'Harry dead?' And he saw the pert lift of her round chin. 'In that case he loses by default. Take me, my chivalrous lover, sweep me away in your white spaceboat.'

He stole a glance at Elfane, became aware of a tart flowering incense she was wearing. Elfane was galvanic with life and thought and wonder. She took life and emotion seriously. Of course Margaret had a lighter touch, an easier laugh, was not intent on killing enemies of her religion. Religion? Joe laughed shortly. Margaret barely recognized the word.

'Why do you laugh?' Elfane asked suspiciously.

'I was thinking of an old friend,' said Joe.

Ballenkarch! A world of fierce gray storms and bright sunlight. A world of blazing color and violent landscape – of rock palisades like walls across the sky – of forests, dim, tall, sequestered – of savannahs ankle-deep in the greenest of grass, coursed by slow mighty rivers. In the low latitudes jungles crowded and jostled, trod under the weaker growths, built up mile after mile of humus until at last the elevation so created acted as a brake on their vitality.

And among the mountain passes, through the forests,

wandering across the plains, rolled the Ballenkart clans in caravans of brightly-painted wains. They were great bull-voiced men in armor of steel and leather, wasting their blood in vendetta and duel.

They lived in an atmosphere of epic — of raids, massacres, fights with tall black jungle bipeds, fearsome and semi-intelligent. For weapons they used swords lances, a portable arbalest which flung fist-size stones. Their language, divorced from the current of galactic civilization a thousand years, was a barely understandable pidgin and they wrote in pictographs.

The *Belsaurion* set down on a green plain drenched in sunlight. In the distance rain hung in veils from a black welter of clouds and a gorgeous rainbow arched over a forest of tall blue-green trees.

A rude pavilion of logs and corrugated metal served as depot and waiting room and when the *Belsaurion* finally shuddered to rest a little wagon with eight creaking wheels came chugging out across the grass, stopped alongside the ship.

Joe asked Hableyat, 'Where is the city?'

Hableyat chuckled. 'The Prince won't allow a ship any closer to his main settlements for fear of slavers. These burly Ballenkarts are much in demand on Frums and Perkins for bodyguards.'

The port was opened to the outdoors. Fresh air, smelling of damp earth, swept into the ship. The steward announced to the saloon, 'Passengers wishing to alight may do so. You are cautioned not to leave the vicinity of the ship until transportation has been arranged to Vail-Alan.'

Joe looked around for Elfane. She was speaking vehemently to the two Druid missionaries and they listened with expressions of mulish obstinacy. Elfane become enraged, jerked away, marched white-faced to the port and outside. The Druids followed, muttering to each other.

Elfane approached the driver of the eight-wheeled vehicle. 'I wish to be conveyed to Vail-Alan at once.'

He looked at her without expression. Hableyat touched her elbow. 'Priestess, an air-car shortly will arrive to convey us a great deal faster than this vehicle.'

She turned, walked swiftly away. Hableyat leaned close to the driver, who whispered a few sentences. Hableyat's face changed in the slightest degree – a twitch of a muscle, a deepening of his jowl-crease. He saw Joe watching, instantly became businesslike and the driver was once more blank-faced.

Hableyat moved off by himself in a preoccupied manner. Joe joined him. 'Well' – sardonically – 'what's the news?'

Hableyat said, 'Very bad – very bad indeed —'

'How so?'

Hableyat hesitated an instant, then blurted in as frank an exhibition of emotion as Joe had seen him express, 'My opponents at home are much stronger with the Lathbon than I knew. Magnerru Ippolito himself is at Vail-Alan. He has reached the Prince and evidently has uttered some unsavory truths regarding the Druids. So now I learn that plans for a Druid cathedral and monastery have been abandoned and that Wanbrion, a Sub-Thearch, is guarded closely.'

In exasperation Joe surveyed the portly Hableyat. 'Well, isn't that what you want? Certainly a Druid advising the Prince wouldn't help the Mangs.'

Hableyat shook his head sadly. 'My friend, you are as easily gulled as my militant countrymen.'

'I suppose I'm dense.'

Hableyat held his hands out from his sides as if revealing all to Joe by the gesture. 'It's so obvious.'

'Sorry.'

'In this manner – the Druids plan to assimilate Ballenkarch to themselves. My opponents on Mangtse, learning of this intent, rush forward to oppose it tooth and nail. They will not consider implications, probable eventualities. No, since it is a Druid scheme it must be countered. And with a program which, in my opinion, will seriously embarrass Mangtse.'

'I see what you're driving at,' said Joe, 'but not how it works.'

Hableyat faced him with an amused expression. 'My dear fellow, human reverence is by no means infinite. I would say that the Kyril Laity lavish the maximum on their Tree. So – what will be the reaction to news of another divine Tree?'

Joe grinned. 'It will cut their reverence toward the first tree in half.'

'Naturally I am unable to estimate the diminution but in any event it will be considerable. Doubt, heresy, will find ears and the Druids will notice that the Laity is no longer unquestioning and innocent. They identify themselves now with the Tree. It is theirs, unique of its kind, solitary in the universe.

'Then – suddenly another Tree exists on Ballenkarch – planted by the Druids and there are rumors that its presence is politically motivated.' He raised his eyebrows expressively.

'But the Druids, by controlling Ballenkarch and these new industries, can still wind up on the credit side.'

Hableyat shook his head. 'My friend, Mangtse is potentially the weakest world of the three. That's the crux of the entire matter. Kyril has its manpower, Ballenkarch has the mineral and agricultural wealth, an aggressive population, a warlike tradition. In any association of worlds Ballenkarch eventually will be the cannibal mate devouring his spouse.

'Think of the Druids – the epicures, the sophisticated masters of five billion slaves. Picture them trying to dominate Ballenkarch. It is laughable. In fifty years the Ballenkarts would be whipping the Thearchs from the gates of Divinal and burning the Tree for a victory bonfire.

'Consider the alternative – Ballenkarch tied to Mangtse. A period of tribulation, profit for none. And now the Druids will have no choice – they will have to buckle down and *work*. With the Ballenkart industries denied them they will of necessity bring new ways to Kyril – factories, industries, education. The old ways will go.

'The Druids might or might not lose the reins of power – but Kyril would remain an integrated industrial unit and there would go the natural market for Mang products. So you see, with the Kyril and Ballenkarch markets both removed our own Mang economy would dwindle, suffer. We would be forced to recover our markets by military action and we might lose.'

'I understand all this,' said Joe slowly, 'but it gets nowhere. Just what do you want?'

'Ballenkarch is self-sufficient. At the moment neither Mangtse nor Kyril can exist alone. We form a natural couple. But as you see the Druids are dissatisfied with the influx of wealth. They demand more and they think to acquire it by controlling the Ballenkarch industries.

'I want to prevent this – and I also want to prevent a Mangtse–Ballenkarch understanding, which would be *prima facie* unnatural. I wish to see a new regime on Kyril, a government committed to improving the productive and purchasing power of the Laity, a government committed to the natural alliance with Mangtse.'

'Too bad the three worlds can't form a common council.'

Hableyat sighed. 'That idea, while felicitous, flies in the face of three realities. First, the current policy of the Druids – second, the ascendancy of the Redbranch on Mangtse – and third, the ambitions of the Prince of Ballenkarch. Change all three of these realities and such a union might be consummated. I for one would approve it – why not?' he mused as if to himself and behind the bland yellow mask Joe glimpsed the face of a very tired man.

'What will happen to you now?'

Hableyat pursed his lips dolefully. 'If my authority actually has been superseded I will be expected to kill myself. Don't look bewildered – it is a Mang custom, a method of underscoring disapproval. I fear I am not long for the world.'

'Why not return to Mangtse and repair your political fences?'

Hableyat shook his head. 'That is not our custom. You may smile but you forget that societies exist through general agreement as to certain symbols, necessities which must be obeyed.'

'Here comes the air-car,' said Joe. 'If I were you, instead of committing suicide, I'd try to work out some kind of scheme to get the Prince on your side. He seems to be the key. They're both after him, Druids and Mangs.'

Hableyat shook his head. 'Not the Prince. He's a queer man, a mixture of bandit, jester and visionary. He seems to regard this new Ballenkarch as an interesting game, a sportive recreation.'

XI

The air-car landed, a big-bellied transport in need of paint. Two large men in red knee-length breeches, loose blue jackets, black caps, swaggered from the air-car, wearing the placidly arrogant expressions of a military élite.

'Lord Prince sends his greetings,' said the first to the Beland officer. 'He understands that there are foreign agents among the passengers, so he will have all who land conveyed before him at once.'

There was no further conversation. Into the car trooped Elfane and Hableyat, the two Druids clutching their portable alter, the Mangs, glaring yellow-eyed at Hableyat, and Joe. These were all for Hableyat — the Cils and the aged woman in the black gown would continue their journey to Castlegran, Cil or Beland and none were discharged from the hold.

Joe crossed the fuselage, dropped into a seat beside Elfane. She turned her head, showed him a face which seemed drained of its youth. 'What do you want with me?'

'Nothing. Are you angry with me?'

'You're a Mang spy.'

Joe laughed uneasily. 'Oh — because I'm thick with Hableyat?'

'What did he send you to tell me now?'

The question took Joe aback. It opened up a vista for speculation. Could it be possible that Hableyat was using him as a means to convey ideas of Hableyat's choosing to the Druids through Elfane?

He said, 'I don't know whether or not he wanted this to reach you. But he explained to me why he's been helping you bring your Tree here and it sounds convincing to me.'

'In the first place,' said Elfane scathingly. 'We have no more Tree. It was stolen from us at Junction.' Her eyes widened and she looked at him with a sudden suspicion. 'Was that your doing too? Is it possible that . . .'

Joe sighed. 'You're determined to think the worst of me. Very well. If you weren't so damned beautiful and appealing I would think twice about you. But you're planning to bust in on the Prince with your two milk-faced Druids and you think you can wind him around your finger. Maybe you can. I know very well you'd stop at nothing. And now I'll get off my chest what Hableyat said and you can do what you like with the information.'

He glared at her, challenging her to speak, but she tossed her head and stared hard out the window.

'He believes that if you succeed in this mission, then you and your Druids will wind up playing second fiddle to these tough Ballenkarts. If you don't succeed – well, the Mangs will probably figure out something unpleasant for you personally but the Druids – according to Hableyat – eventually will come out ahead.'

'Go away,' she said in a choked voice. 'All you do is scare me. Go away.'

'Elfane – forget all this Druid-Mang-Tree-of-Life stuff and I'll take you back to Earth. That is if I get off the planet alive.'

She showed him the back of her head. The car buzzed, vibrated, rose into the air. The landscape dished out below them. Massive mountains shot and marbled with snow and ice, luxuriant meadowland with grass glowing the sharp bright color of prismatic green, spread below.

106

They crossed the range. The car jerked, jolted in bumpy air, slanted down toward an inland sea.

A settlement, obviously raw and new, had grown up on the shore of this sea. Three heavy docks, a dozen large rectangular buildings — glass sided, roofed with bright metal — formed the heart of the town. A mile beyond a promontory covered with trees overlooked the sea and in the shadow of this promontory the car grounded.

The door opened. One of the Ballenkarts motioned brusquely. 'This way.'

Joe followed Elfane to the ground and saw ahead a long low building with a glass front looking across the vista of sea and plain. The Ballenkart corporal made another peremptory motion. 'To the Residence,' he said curtly.

Resentfully Joe started for the building, thinking that these soldiers made poor emissaries of good will. His nerves tautened as he walked. The atmosphere was hardly one of welcome. The tension, he noticed, gripped everyone. Elfane moved as if her legs were rigid. Erru Kametin's jaw shone bright yellow along the bone line.

At the rear Joe noticed Hableyat speaking urgently with the two Druid missionaries. They seemed reluctant. Hableyat raised his voice. Joe heard him say, 'What's the difference? This way you at least have a chance, whether you distrust my motives or not.' The Druids at last appeared to acquiesce. Hableyat marched briskly ahead and said in a loud voice, 'Halt! This impudence must not go on!'

The two Ballenkarts swung around in amazement. With a stern face Hableyat said, 'Go, get your master. We will suffer this indignity no longer.'

The Ballenkarts blinked, slightly crestfallen to find their authority questioned. Erru Kametin, eyes snapping,

107

said, 'What are you saying, Hableyat? Are you trying to compromise us in the eyes of the Prince?'

Hableyat said, 'He must learn that we Mangs prize our dignities. We will not stir from this ground until he advances to greet us in the manner of a courteous host.'

Erru Kametin laughed scornfully. 'Stay then.' He flung his scarlet cloak about him, turned, proceeded toward the Residence. The Ballenkarts conferred and one accompanied the Mangs. The other eyed Hableyat with truculent eyes. 'Wait until the Prince hears of this!'

The rest had rounded a corner. Hableyat leisurely drew his hand from his cloak, discharged a tube at the guard. The guard's eyes became milky, he tumbled to the ground.

'He's merely stunned,' said Hableyat to Joe, who had turned protestingly. To the Druids, 'Hurry.'

Lifting their robes they ran to a nearby bank of soft dirt. One dug a hole with a stick, the other opened the altar, tenderly lifted out the miniature Tree. A small pot surrounded its roots.

Joe heard Elfane gasp. 'You two —'

'Silence,' rapped Hableyat. 'Attend your own concerns if you are wise. These are Arch-Thearchs, both of them.'

'Manaolo – a dupe!'

Into the hole went the roots. Soil was patted firm. The Druids closed the altar, dusted off their hands, and once more became empty-faced monks. And the Son of the Tree stood firm in the ground of Ballenkarch, bathing in the hot yellow light. Unless one looked closely, it was merely another young shrub.

'Now,' said Hableyat placidly, 'we continue to the Residence.'

Elfane glared at Hableyat and the Druids, her eyes flaming with rage and humiliation. 'All this time you've been laughing at me!'

'No, no, Priestess,' said Hableyat. 'Calmness, I implore you. You'll need all your wits when you face the Prince. Believe me, you served a very useful function.'

Elfane turned blindly as if to run off toward the sea but Joe caught hold of her. For a moment she stared into his eyes, her muscles like wire. Then she relaxed, grew limp. 'Very well, I'll go in.'

They continued, meeting halfway a squad of six soldiers evidently sent out to escort them in. No one heeded the numb form of the guard.

At the portal they were subjected to a search, quick but so detailed and thorough as to evoke angry protests from the Druids and an outraged yelp from Elfane. The arsenal so discovered was surprising – hand-conics from each of the Druids, Hableyat's stun-tube and a collapsible dagger, Joe's gun, a little polished tube Elfane carried in her sleeve.

The corporal stood back, gestured. 'You are permitted to enter the Residence. See that you observe the accepted forms of respect.'

Passing through an antechamber painted with grotesque half-demoniac animals they entered a large hall. The ceiling beams were great timbers, hand-hewn and notched into a formalized pattern, the walls were surfaced with woven rattan. At either side banks of green and red plants lined the wall and the floor was covered by a soft rug of fiber woven and dyed in a striking pattern of scarlet, black and green.

Opposite the entrance was a dais, flanked by two heavy balustrades of rust-red wood, and a wide throne-like seat of the same russet wood. At the moment the throne was empty.

Twenty or thirty men stood about the room – large,

sun-tanned, some with bristling mustaches — awkward and ill at ease as if unused to a roof over their heads. All wore red knee-length breeches. Some wore blouses of various colors while others were bare-chested with capes of black fur slung back from their shoulders. All bore short heavy sabers in their belts and all eyed the new-comers without friendliness.

Joe looked from face to face. Harry Creath would not be far from Vail-Alan, the center of activity. But he was not in the hall.

Beside the dais in a group stood the Redbranch Mangs. Erru Kametin spoke in a harsh staccato to the woman. The two proctors listening silently, half-turned away.

A house-marshal with a long brass clarion stepped into the room, blew a brilliant fanfare. Joe smiled faintly. Like a musical comedy — warriors in bright uniforms, pageantry, pomp, punctilio . . .

The fanfare again — *tantara-tantivy* — shrill, exciting.

'The Prince of Vail-Alan! Ruler Preemptor across the face of Ballenkarch!'

A blond man, slight beside the Ballenkarts, stepped briskly up on the dais, seated himself on the throne. He had a round bony face with lines of humor around his mouth, nervous twitching hands, an air of gay intelligence, reckless impatience. From the crowd came a hoarse '*Aaaaah*' of reverence.

Joe nodded slowly without surprise. Who else?

Harry Creath flicked his eyes around the room. They rested on Joe, passed, swung back. For a minute he stared in amazement.

'*Joe Smith!* What in Heaven's name are you doing out here?'

110

This was the moment he had come a thousand light years for. And now Joe's mind refused to function correctly. He stuttered the words he had rehearsed for two years, through toil, danger, boredom — the words which expressed the two-year obsession — 'I came out to get you.'

He had said them, he was vindicated. The compulsion which was almost auto-suggestion had been allayed. But the words had been spoken and Harry's mobile face expressed astonishment. 'Out here? All the way — to get me?'

'That's right.'

'Get me to do what?' Harry leaned back and his wide mouth broke into a grin.

'Well — you left some unfinished business on Earth.'

'None that I know of. You'd have to talk long and fast to get me in motion.' He turned to a tall guard with a face like a rock. 'Have these people been searched for weapons?'

'Yes, Prince.'

Harry turned back to Joe with a grimace of jocular apology. 'There's too many people interested in me. I can't ignore the obvious risks. Now, you were saying — you want me to go back to Earth. Why?'

Why? Joe asked himself the question. *Why?* Because Margaret thought herself in love with Harry and Joe thought she was in love with a dream. Because Joe thought that if Margaret could know Harry for a month, rather than for two days, if she could see him in day-to-day living, if she could realize that love was not a series of lifts and thrills like a roller-coaster ride — that marriage was not a breathless round of escapades.

In short, if Margaret's pretty frivolous head could be rattled loose from its nonsense — then there would be

111

room in it for Joe. Was that it? It had seemed easy, flung out to Mars for Harry only to find Harry had departed for Io. And from Io to Pluto, the Jumping-off Place. And then the compulsion began to take hold, the doggedness. Out from Pluto, on and on and on. Then Kyril, then Junction, now Ballenkarch.

Joe blushed, intensely aware of Elfane at his back, watching him with bright-eyed speculation. He opened his mouth to speak, closed it again. *Why?*

Eyes were on him, eyes from all over the room. Curious eyes, cold uninterested eyes, hostile eyes, searching eyes – Hableyat's placid, Elfane's probing, Harry Creath's mocking eyes. And into Joe's confused mind one hard fact emerged – he would be displaying himself as the most consummate ass in the history of the universe if he told the truth.

'Something to do with Margaret?' asked Harry mercilessly. 'She send you out here?'

Joe saw Margaret as if in a vision, inspecting the two of them derisively. His eyes swung to Elfane. A hellion, obstinate, intolerant, too intense and full of life for her own good. But sincere and decent.

'Margaret?' Joe laughed. 'No. Nothing to do with Margaret. In fact I've changed my mind. Keep to hell away from Earth.'

Harry relaxed slightly. 'If it had to do with Margaret – why, you're rather outdated.' He craned his neck. 'Where the devil is she? *Margaret!*'

'Margaret?' muttered Joe.

She stepped up on the dais beside Harry. 'Hello, Joe' – as if she'd taken leave of him yesterday afternoon – 'what a nice surprise.'

She was laughing inside, very quietly. Joe grinned also, grimly. Very well, he'd take his medicine. He met their eyes, said, 'Congratulations.' It occurred to him that Margaret was in sheer fact living the life she claimed she wanted to lead – excitement, intrigue, adventure. And it seemed to agree with her.

XII

Harry had been speaking to him. Joe suddenly became aware of his voice. '— You see, Joe, this is a wonderful thing we're doing out here, a wonderful world. It's busting open with high-grade ore, timber, organic produce, manpower. I've got a picture in my mind, Joe – Utopia.

'There's a good bunch of lads behind me, and we're working together. They're a little rough yet but they see this world the way I see it and they're willing to take a chance on me. To begin with, of course, I had to knock a few heads together but they know who's boss now and we're getting on fine.' Harry looked fondly over the crowd of Ballenkarts, any one of whom could have strangled him with one hand.

'In another twenty years,' said Harry, 'you won't believe your eyes. What we're going to do to the planet! it's marvelous, I tell you, Joe. Excuse me now, for a few minutes. There's affairs of state.' He settled himself into his chair, looked from Mangs to Druids.

'We might as well talk it over now. I see it's all fresh and ripe in your minds. There's my old friend Hableyat.' He winked at Joe. 'Foxy Grandpa. What's the occasion, Hableyat?'

Hableyat strutted forward. 'Your Excellency, I find myself in a peculiar position. I have not communicated with my home government and I am not sure as to the extent of my authority.'

Harry said to a guard. 'Find the Magnerru.' To Hableyat, 'Magnerru Ippolito is fresh from Mangtse and he claims to speak with the voice of your Ampianu General.'

From an archway to the side a Mang approached – a sturdy square-faced Mang with the brightest of black eyes, a lemon-yellow skin, bright orange lips. He wore a scarlet robe embroidered with a border of purple and green squares, a cubical black hat.

Erru Kametin and the other Mangs of his party bowed deeply, saluting with outflung arms. Hableyat nodded respectfully, a fixed smile on his plump lips.

'Magnerru,' said Prince Harry, 'Hableyat wants to know the extent of his freedom to make policy.'

'None,' rasped the Magnerru. 'None whatever. Hableyat and the Bluewaters have been discredited in the Ampianu, the Lathbon sits with the Redbranch. Hableyat speaks with no voice but his own and it will soon be stilled.'

Harry nodded. 'Then it will be wise to hear, before his demise, what his views are.'

'My Lord,' said Hableyat, his face still frozen in its jovial mask, 'my words are trivial. I prefer to hear the enunciations of the Magnerru and of the two Arch-Thearchs we have with us. My Lord, I may state that the highest of Kyril face you – Arch-Thearchs Oporeto Implan and Gameanza. They will ably present their views.'

'My modest residence is thick with celebrities,' said Harry.

Gameanza stepped forward with a glittering glance for the Magnerru. 'Prince Harry, I consider the present atmosphere unsuited to discussion of policy. Whenever the Prince desires – the sooner the better – I will communicate to him the trend of Druid policy together with my views in regard to the political and ethical situation.'

The Magnerru said, 'Talk to the dry-mouthed slug. Listen to his efforts to fix the slave system on Ballen-

116

karch. Then send him back to his fetid gray world in the hold of a cattle ship.'

Gameanza stiffened. His skin seemed to become brittle. He said to Harry in a sharp brassy voice, 'I am at your pleasure.'

Harry rose to his feet. 'Very well, we'll retire for half an hour and discuss your proposals.' He raised a hand to the Magnerru. 'You'll have the same privilege, so be patient. Talk over old times with Hableyat. I understand he formerly occupied your position.'

Arch-Thearch Gameanza followed him as he jumped from the dais and left the hall and after moved the Arch-Thearch Oporeto Implan. Margaret waved a casual hand to Joe. 'See you later.' She slipped away through another door.

Joe found a bench to the side of the room, wearily seated himself. Before him like a posed tableau stood the rigid Mangs, the exquisite wisp of flesh that was Elfane, Hableyat – suddenly gone vague and helpless – the Ballenkarts in their gorgeous costumes, troubled, confused, unused to the bickering of sharp wits, glancing uneasily at each other over heavy shoulders, muttering.

Elfane turned her head, gazed around the room. She saw Joe, hesitated, then crossed the floor, seated herself beside him. After a moment she said haughtily, 'You're laughing at me – mocking me.'

'I wasn't aware of it.'

'You've found the man you were seeking,' she said with eyebrows arched. 'Why don't you do something?'

Joe shrugged. 'I've changed my mind.'

'Because that yellow-haired woman – Margaret – is here?'

'Partly.'

'You never mentioned her to me.'

'I had no idea you'd be interested.'

Elfane looked stonily across the audience hall. Joe said, 'Do you know why I changed my mind?'

She shook her head. 'No. I don't.'

'It's because of you.'

Elfane turned back with glowing eyes. 'So it *was* the blonde woman who brought you out here.'

Joe sighed. 'Every man can be a damn fool once in his life. At *least* once . . .'

She was not appeased. 'Now, I suppose, if I sent you to look for someone you wouldn't go? That she meant more to you than I do?'

Joe groaned. 'Oh Lord! In the first place you've never given me any reason to think that you – oh, hell!'

'I offered to let you be my lover.'

Joe eyed her with exasperation. 'I'd like to . . .' He recalled that Kyril was not Earth, that Elfane was a Priestess, not a college girl.

Elfane laughed. 'I understand you very well, Joe. On Earth men are accustomed to having their own way and the women are auxiliary inhabitants. And don't forget, Joe, you've never told *me* anything – that you loved me.'

Joe growled, 'I've been afraid to.'

'Try me.'

Joe tried and the happy knowledge came to him that, in spite of a thousand light-years and two extremes of culture, girls were girls. Priestesses or co-eds.

Harry and the Arch-Druid Gameanza returned to the room and a set expression hung like a frame on the Druid's white face. Harry said to the Magnerru, 'Perhaps you will be good enough to exchange a few words with me?'

The Magnerru clapped his hands in repressed anger against his robe, followed Harry into the inner chambers. Evidently the informal approach found no responsive chord in him.

Hableyat settled beside Joe. Elfane looked stonily to one side. Hableyat wore a worried expression. His yellow jowls hung flaccid, the eyelids drooped over his eyes.

Joe said, 'Cheer up, Hableyat, you're not dead yet.'

Hableyat shook his head. 'The schemes of my entire life are toppling into fragments.'

Joe looked at him sharply. Was the gloom exaggerated, the sighs over-doleful? He said guardedly, 'I have yet to learn your positive program.'

Hableyat shrugged. 'I am a patriot. I wish to see my planet prosperous, waxing in wealth. I am a man imbued with the culture of my world; I can conceive of no better way of life, and I wish to see this culture expand, enriching itself with the cultures of other worlds, adapting the good, overcoming the bad.'

'In other words,' said Joe. 'You're as strenuous an imperialist as your military friends. Only your methods are different.'

'I'm afraid you have defined me,' sighed Hableyat. 'Furthermore I fear that in this era military imperialism is almost impossible – that cultural imperialism is the only practicable form. A planet cannot be successfully subjugated and occupied from another planet. It may be devastated, laid waste, but the logistics of conquest are practically insuperable. I fear that the adventures proposed by the Redbranch will exhaust Mang, ruin Ballenkarch and make the way easy for a Druid religious imperialism.'

Joe felt Elfane stiffen. 'Why is that worse than Mang cultural imperialism?'

'My dear Priestess,' said Hableyat, 'I could never argue cogently enough to convince you. I will say one word – that the Druids produce very little with a vast potentiality – that they live on the backs of a groaning mass – and that I hope the system is never extended to

119

include me among the Laity.'

'Me, either,' said Joe.

Elfane jumped to her feet. 'You're both vile!'

Joe surprised himself by reaching, pulling her back beside him with a thud. She struggled a moment, then subsided.

'Lesson number one in Earth culture,' said Joe cheerfully. 'It's bad manners to argue religion.'

A soldier burst into the chamber, panting, his face twisted in terror. 'Horrible – out along the road ... Where's the Prince? Get the Prince – a terrible growth!'

Hableyat jumped to his feet, his face sharp alert. He ran nimbly out the door and after a second Joe said, 'I'm going too.'

Elfane, without a word, followed.

Joe had a flash impression of complete confusion. A milling mob of men circled an object he could not identify – a squat green-and-brown thing which seemed to writhe and heave.

Hableyat burst through the circle, with Joe at his side and Elfane pressing at Joe's back. Joe looked in wonder. The Son of the Tree?

It had grown, become complicated. No longer did it resemble the Kyril Tree. The Son had adapted itself to a new purpose – protection, growth, flexibility.

It reminded Joe of a tremendous dandelion. A white fuzzy ball held itself twenty feet above the ground on a slender swaying stalk, surrounded by an inverted cone of flat green fronds. At the base of each front a green tendril, streaked and speckled with black, thrust itself out. Clasped in these tendrils were the bodies of three men.

Hableyat squawked, 'The thing's a devil,' and clapped his hand to his pouch. But his weapon had been impounded by the Residence guards.

A Ballenkarch chieftain, his pale face distorted, charged the Son, hacking with his saber. The fuzzy ball swayed toward him a trifle, the tendrils jerked back like the legs of an insect, then snapped in from all sides, wrapped the man close, pierced his flesh. He bawled, fell silent, stiffened. The tendrils flushed red, pulsed, and the Son grew taller.

Four more Ballenkarts, acting in grim concert, charged the Son, six others followed. The tendrils thrust, snapped and ten bodies lay stiff and white on the ground. The Son expanded as if it were being magnified.

Prince Harry's light assured voice said, 'Step aside . . . Now then, step aside.'

Harry stood looking at the plant — twenty feet to the top of the fronds while the fuzzy ball reared another ten above them.

The Son pounced, with a cunning quasi-intelligence. Tendrils unfurled, trapped a dozen roaring men, dragged them close. And now the crowd went wild, swayed back and forth in alternate spasms of rage and fear, at last charged in a screeching melee.

Sabres glittered, swung, chopped. Overhead the fuzzy white ball swung unhurriedly. It was sensate, it saw, felt, planned with a vegetable consciousness, calm, fearless, single-purposed. Its tendrils snaked, twisted, squeezed, returned to drain. And the Son of the Tree soared, swelled.

Panting survivors of the crowd fell back, staring helplessly at the corpse-strewn ground. Harry motioned to one of his personal guard. 'Bring out a heat-gun.'

The Arch-Thearchs came forward, protesting. 'No, no, that is the Sacred Shoot, the Son of the Tree.'

Harry paid them no heed. Gameanza clutched his arm with panicky insistence. 'Recall your soldiers. Feed it nothing but criminals and slaves. In ten years it will be

121

tremendous, a magnificent Tree.'

Harry shook him off, jerked his head at a soldier. 'Take this maniac away.'

A projector on wheels was trundled from behind the Residence, halted fifty feet from the Son. Harry nodded. A thick white beam of energy spat against the Son. *'Aaah!'* sighed the crowd, in near-voluptuous gratification. The exultant sigh stopped short. The Son drank in the energy like sunshine, expanded, luxuriated and grew. A hundred feet the fuzzy white ball towered.

'Turn it against the top,' said Harry anxiously.

The bar of energy swung up the slender stalk, concentrated on the head of the plant. It coruscated, spattered, ducked away.

'It doesn't like it!' cried Harry. *'Pour it on!'*

The Arch-Thearchs, restrained in the rear, howled in near-personal anguish. *'No, no, no!'*

The white ball steadied, spat back a gout of energy. The projector exploded, blasting heads and arms and legs in every direction.

There was a sudden dead silence. Then the moans began. Then sudden screaming as the tendrils snapped forth to feed.

Joe dragged Elfane back and a tendril missed her by a foot. 'But I am a Druid Priestess,' she said in dull astonishment. 'The Tree protects the Druids. The Tree accepts only the lay pilgrims.'

'Pilgrims!' Joe remembered the Kyril pilgrims – tired, dusty, footsore, sick – entering the portal into the Tree. He remembered the pause at the portal, the one last look out across the gray land and up into the foliage before they turned and entered the trunk. Young and old, in all conditions, thousands every day . . .

Joe now had to crane his neck to see the top of the

122

Son. The flexible central shoot was stiffening, the little white ball swung and twisted and peered over its new domain.

Harry came limping up beside Joe, his face a white mask. 'Joe – that's the ungodliest creature I've seen on thirty-two planets.'

'I've seen a bigger one – on Kyril. It eats the citizens by the thousand.'

Harry said, 'These people trust me. They think I'm some kind of god myself – merely because I know a little Earth engineering. I've got to kill that abomination.'

'You're not throwing in with the Druids then?'

Harry sneered. 'What kind of patsy do you take me for, Joe? I'm not throwing in with either one of 'em. A plague on both their houses. I've been holding 'em off, teasing 'em until I could get things straightened out. I'm still not satisfied – but I certainly didn't bargain for something like this. Who the hell brought the thing here?'

Joe was silent. Elfane said, 'It was brought from Kyril by order of the Tree.'

Harry stared. 'My God, does the thing talk too?'

Elfane said vaguely, 'The College of Thearchs reads the will of the Tree by various signs.'

Joe scratched his chin.

'Hmph,' said Harry. 'Fancy decoration for a nice tight little tyranny. But that's not the problem. This thing's got to be killed!' And he muttered, 'I'd like to get the main beast too, just for luck.'

Joe heard – he looked at Elfane expecting to see her flare into anger. But she stood silent, looking at the Son.

Harry said, 'It seems to thrive on energy ... Heat's out. A bomb? Let's try blasting. I'll send down to the warehouse for some splat.'

Gameanza tore himself loose, came running up with

123

his gray robe flapping around his legs. 'Excellency, we vehemently protest your aggressions against this Tree!'

'Sorry,' said Harry, grinning sardonically. 'I call it a murderous beast.'

'It's presence is symbolic of the ties between Kyril and Ballenkarch,' pleaded Gameanza.

'Symbolic my ankle. Clear that metaphysical rubbish out of your mind, man. That thing's a man-killer and I won't have it at large. I pity you for the king-size monster you've got on your own rock – although I suppose I shouldn't.' He looked Gameanza up and down. 'You've made pretty good use of the Tree. It's been your meal ticket for a thousand years. Well, this one is on its way out. In another ten minutes it'll be an acre of splinters.'

Gameanza whirled on his heel, marched twenty feet away, where he conversed in low tones with Oporeto Implan. Ten pounds of explosive, packed with a detonator was heaved against the Son's heavy trunk. Harry raised the radiation gun which would project trigger-frequencies.

On sudden thought, Joe jerked forward, caught his arm. 'Just a minute. Suppose you make an acre of splinters – and each one of the splinters starts to grow?'

Harry put down the projector. 'That's a grisly thought.'

Joe gestured around the countryside. 'All these farms, they look well taken care of, modern.'

'Latest Earth techniques. So what?'

'You don't let your bully-boys pull all the weeds by hand?'

'Of course not. We've got a dozen different weed-killers – hormones . . .' He stopped short, clapped Joe on the shoulder. 'Weed-killers! *Growth* hormones! Joe, I'll make you Secretary of Agriculture!'

'First,' said Joe, 'let's see if the stuff works on the Tree. If it's a vegetable it'll go crazy.'

The Son of the Tree went crazy.

The tendrils twined, contorted, snapped. The fuzzy white head spat chattering arcs of energy in random directions.

The fronds hoisted to a grotesque two hundred feet in seconds, flopped to the ground.

Another heat projector was brought. Now the Son resisted only weakly. The trunk charred; the fronds crisped, blackened.

In minutes the Son of the Tree was an evil-smelling stump.

Prince Harry sat on his throne. The Arch-Thearchs Gameanza and Oporeto Implan stood with pallid faces muffled in their cowls. The Redbranch Mangs waited in a group to the side of the hall in a rigid system of precedence – first the Magnerru in his chased cuirass and scarlet robe, then Erru Kametin and behind him the two proctors.

Harry said in his light clear voice, 'I haven't much to announce – except that for some months now there's been a widespread uncertainty as to which way Ballenkarch is going to jump – toward Mang or toward Kyril.

'Well,' he shifted in his seat, put his hands along the arms of his throne, 'the speculation has been entirely in the minds of the Druids and the Mangs, there was never any indecision here on Ballenkarch. Once and for all we will team up with neither planet.

'We'll develop in a different direction and I believe we'll end up with the finest world this side of Earth. Insofar as the Son of the Tree is concerned I hold no one personally responsible. You Druids acted, I believe,

125

according to your best lights. You're victims of your beliefs, almost as much as your Laity.

'Another thing — while we won't enter any political commitments we're in business. We'll trade. We're building tools — hammers, saws, wrenches, welders. In a year we'll start building electrical equipment. In five years we'll have a spaceyard down there on the shore of Lake Alan.

'In ten years we'll be running our cargo to every star you can see in the night and maybe a few more. So — Magnerru, you can return and convey my message to your Ampianu General and the Lathbon. As for you Druids I doubt if you'll wish to return. There might be quite some turmoil on Kyril by the time you'd arrive.'

Gameanza asked sharply, 'How is that?'

Harry's mouth twitched. 'Call it a guess.'

From Harry's private sundeck, the water of Lake Alan glowed in a thousand shades of sunset. Joe sat in a chair. Beside him sat Elfane, in a simple white gown.

Harry paced up and down, talking, gesticulating, boasting. New reduction furnaces at Palinth, a hundred new schools, power units for the new farmer class, guns for his army.

'They've still got that barbarian streak,' said Harry. 'They love fighting, they love the wildness, their spring festivals, their night fire-dancing. It's born and bred into 'em and I couldn't take it out of 'em if I tried.'

He winked at Joe.

'The fire-breathers I send out against the clans of Vail Macrombie — that's the other continent. I kill two birds with one stone. They work off all their belligerence against the Macrombie cannibals and they're gradually winning the continent. It's bloody, yes — but it fills a need in their souls.

'The young ones we'll bring up differently. Their heroes will be the engineers rather than the soldiers and everything should work out about the same time. The new generation will grow up while their fathers are mopping up along Matenda Cape.'

'Very ingenious,' said Joe. 'And speaking of ingenuity where's Hableyat? I haven't seen him for a day or so.'

Harry dropped into a chair. 'Hableyat's gone.'

'Gone? Where?'

'Officially, I don't know – especially since we have Druids among us.'

Elfane stirred.

'I'm – no longer a Druid. I've torn it out of me. Now I'm a' – she looked up at Joe – 'a what?'

'An expatriate,' said Joe. 'A space-waif. A woman without a country.' He looked back to Harry. 'Less of the mystery. It can't be that important.'

'But it is! Maybe.'

Joe shrugged. 'Suit yourself.'

'No,' said Harry, 'I'll tell you. Hableyat, as you know, is in disgrace. He's out and the Magnerru Ippolito is in. Mang politics are complex and cryptic but they seem to hinge a great deal on prestige – on face. The Magnerru lost face here on Ballenkarch. If Hableyat can perform some remarkable feat he'll be back in the running. And so it's to our advantage to have the Bluewaters in power on Mangtse.'

'Well?'

'I gave Hableyat all the anti-weed hormone we had – about five tons of it. He had it loaded into a ship I made available to him and took off.' Harry made a whimsical gesture. 'Where he's going – I don't know.'

Elfane hissed softly under her breath, shivered, looked away out over Lake Alan, pink, gold, lavender,

127

turquoise in the sunset. 'The Tree . . .'

Harry rose to his feet. 'Time for dinner. If that's his plan — to spray the Tree with hormone — it should be quite a show.'